If only he could experience the ultimate high...If only he could stave off the pangs of withdrawal... If only he could keep one step ahead of the law... If only...

Although the circumstances may be different, Lefty's search for lasting satisfaction—and the dark avenues he explored—are familiar paths for quite a few of us. LEFTY will grip you with a dramatic, true-to-life story of that search. More importantly, LEFTY will surprise you with the life-and-death decision that turned the tide for a desperate young junkie...and can do the same for you.

BY John Benton

Lefty

JOHN BENTON

NEW HOPE
BOOKS

Fleming H. Revell Company
Old Tappan, New Jersey

Scripture quotation in this volume is from the King James Version of the Bible.

ISBN: 0-8007-8401-4
A New Hope Book
Copyright © 1981 by John Benton
All rights reserved
Printed in the United States of America

This is an original New Hope Book, published by New Hope Books, a division of Fleming H. Revell Company, Old Tappan, New Jersey.

Lefty

1

I glanced furtively up the street. Instinctively my fingers tightened on the chain I gripped in my left hand. Then I saw him—the old man shuffling along toward me. Easy. He would be my next victim.

I leaned up against a telephone pole and looked the other way so he wouldn't suspect. I whistled and began to casually twirl the length of chain I held. Out of the corner of my eye I could see that the old man was still shuffling my way. Poor guy. He had no idea what was about to befall him!

I was almost eighteen, strong as an ox and agile as a deer. I had to be, to survive in this ghetto. So why should somebody like me pick on a tottering old man? Well, why not? I had to have my drugs. After all, it had been almost six hours—since early morning—since I had gotten off, and I would soon be getting sick. I had to score—and do it quickly.

The old man stopped about fifteen feet from me and looked uneasily in my direction. Did he suspect something? I knew he did, because from where I was standing, I could almost see his knees knocking together. Trying to make it look as though he had just remembered some business he had to attend to in the other direction, he turned and started to walk away.

No way was my prey going to get away from me! I sprang like a tiger to cover the distance between us, my chain ready. I was going to come down hard and wrap it around his neck. My heavy chain, with its thick links, would circle around his neck a couple of times and choke all the resistance out of him.

It always worked. And people were so terrified, they didn't have a chance to react or to scream. It was the best weapon I had ever used, and I was one of the best in using it.

I gritted my teeth and tightened my grip on the chain. About three feet of chain hung in front of my left hand. I was so close now that I raised it over my head and began to twirl it.

I'd made quite a name for myself in my ghetto neighborhood. I guess people easily recognized me because I was so adept with my left hand. Besides, no one else I knew handled a chain left-handed. I guess that made me easier to remember. That was both good and bad. Good when I wanted to make the neighborhood afraid. Bad if somebody dared squeal on me to the cops.

Ready for the "kill," I stretched to my full five feet eight inches. Every muscle in my body cooperated. This was it!

Then, "Raisin bread! Raisin bread!" someone screamed from atop a nearby tenement roof.

I recognized the warning, but it came almost too late. The momentum of the chain was going to be difficult to stop. So I threw myself to the sidewalk, and the chain came crashing down beside me. Its force rolled me over, and I landed in the filthy gutter.

When I looked up, the old man was standing over me, concern written all over his face.

"Hey, young feller," he said in a creaky voice, "what are you doing down there in the gutter?"

I was shaking so badly I could hardly answer. But I kept my wits about me enough to reply, "Mister, my dog was

running loose, and I thought I spotted him just up there
ahead of you. I jumped forward, but this dumb chain for
my dog caught me around the legs and tangled me all up.
The next thing I knew I was here in this filthy gutter. But I
don't think I'm hurt. Maybe a few scratches. Nothing serious. Don't worry about me."

He looked at me skeptically, and I continued, "I suppose
that dumb dog took off and headed for One Hundred
Twenty-fifth Street."

The old man laughed. I wondered whether he had any
idea what I was about to do. Maybe his partner had warned
him.

I got up, hurriedly brushed the worst of the dirt off, and
took off running the other way. I kept my ear turned in his
direction in case he fired a warning shot.

Half a block away I looked up. Peering over the tenement roof was a buddy, Oscar Rodriguez. He clenched his
fist and raised it high in the air. I didn't dare signal back. In
fact, I was too shook to do anything! I had almost mugged a
decoy cop!

I ran to the end of the block and up Madison Avenue,
where I slipped inside a tenement house to catch my
breath. That sure was a close one. Maybe someday I could
pay Oscar back the favor.

He always seemed to be able to spot the cops. The signal
in the neighborhood was either "Raisin bread" or "Eliot
Ness." That told us the cops were around.

Of course, Oscar was older and wiser. I guess he was
about twenty-three. He had done time in Attica Prison. So
he knew a lot of the tricks—including the tricks of the cops.

There was so much crime in our neighborhood that the
cops had started a new enforcement program. They were
continually appearing as decoys—such as little old ladies or

old men—like the one I had almost mugged. They'd have a backup partner to help them. And would you believe they sometimes even dressed as ministers?

I waited inside about ten minutes and stepped gingerly out into the street again. Oscar was down at the corner and came running as soon as he saw me.

"Lefty," he said before I even had a chance to thank him, "you have to be more careful. I've been following that decoy cop all the way along the street. Do you know who that is you almost mugged?"

"I have no idea at all."

"That was McGinnis."

"McGinnis? Boy, oh, boy! I had no idea that was McGinnis. I was this close to him"—I measured the distance with my hands—"and I couldn't tell that was McGinnis. These decoy cops are really into it, aren't they? I swear McGinnis looked eighty years old."

We stood there chatting for a couple of minutes. Then we heard someone ask, "Hey, do you guys know where I can buy some drugs?"

We both spun around to face a clean-looking young kid. His kind were coming into our neighborhood a lot these days. These kids were from outside New York City and came into Spanish Harlem to buy their drugs. Small communities were really tough on pushers. It seemed as though everybody knew everybody else and what was going on. But in New York City, the drug pushers seemed to be everywhere, and nobody knew their business. It was easy for them to hide when the heat was on.

Oscar studied the kid carefully. Then he replied, "Yeah, I know where you can get the best stuff in the city. How much money do you have?"

"Sixty bucks," he answered.

My mind went into high gear. I still had my chain

wrapped around my left hand, and I had a strong impulse to let the kid have it right then. If he said he had sixty bucks, he probably had a lot more than that. I knew how these guys operated. They usually had five hundred dollars or a thousand dollars tucked on them somewhere. But something restrained me from letting him have it. He seemed so innocent. And he was really brave to come to 110th Street and Madison Avenue. Some said it was the most notorious part of the city.

"Let's see your money, kid," Oscar said.

The boy pulled out three twenties. Oscar grabbed them and said, "All right, tell you what I'll do. You stay right here, and I'll be right back with the dope."

"But you have my money," the kid protested.

"Look," Oscar replied, "my connection doesn't want any strangers coming around. So it has to be my way—or no way at all. You want your money back?"

The kid shook his head. "I have to have some drugs," he replied. "You look like people I can trust."

I swallowed to keep from laughing out loud. No junkie ever trusted another junkie. This kid was so naive that he had to be easy pickings.

"Tell you what, Oscar," I said. "You go get the man's drugs, and I'll wait here with him. That way he won't have to worry."

As soon as Oscar was out of sight, I planned to wrap my chain around the kid's neck. I knew he had more money on him. Probably credit cards, too.

Oscar surprised me when he responded, "No, Lefty, I think you'd better come with me."

"Now, Oscar," I protested, "I know your connection might not even want me around. So I think I'd better just stay here."

Oscar shook his head vigorously.

Somehow I had to get Oscar to go alone. He might have been smart on that police decoy, but I sure wished he'd move off and let me at this kid.

Before I knew it, Oscar had my arm and was pulling me along after him. Angrily, I pushed him away.

"For crying out loud, Lefty, I need you to go with me," Oscar said. "Don't you understand what I'm trying to tell you? I mean, I have to walk into this tenement house, and anybody might be able to get me. I need protection." He lowered his voice. "Protection like that chain around your hand. Understand?"

Of course I didn't understand. Oscar could take care of himself. Maybe he didn't understand that I was starting to get sick and that I needed some money to get off. Now he wanted me to go with him to buy drugs for this dumb kid. I was getting madder and madder.

Oscar was so persistent that I decided to go with him—at least until we got around the corner. Then I could tell him what I had in mind and work a deal with him. I would split half of what I got from mugging the kid; Oscar could keep the sixty bucks. So I finally said, "Okay, Oscar, if you insist. I certainly want you to come back with some good stuff for this man."

"Stay right here," Oscar told the kid. "It should take only fifteen to twenty minutes. But whatever you do, don't follow us. The connection I have is a real screamer. If he finds out we've been followed, that'll be the end of you and me and Lefty. Get it?"

The kid's eyes widened, but he nodded.

When Oscar and I got around the corner, I grabbed his arm and dragged him to a halt.

"For crying out loud, Oscar, don't you know that that kid is an easy setup? He's probably from New Jersey and loaded with money. I'm going to go back and wrap him with my chain. I'll bet his pockets are loaded with dough. You stupid nut; why did you make me come with you?"

Oscar began to laugh. "Lefty, I just don't know what I'm going to do about you! Here, just a few minutes ago, I saved you from jail by warning you of that decoy cop. And so help me, you almost got yourself right back into trouble again. When are you ever going to learn? Couldn't you see what was happening?"

"Of course I saw what was happening. I also noticed a big bulge in that pocket he pulled the money from. I'll bet he's got a wad of money. You'd better believe I know what's happening."

Oscar laughed again. "Lefty, I'm going to have to teach you a big, big lesson. Come on."

We headed down the block, but I had no idea what Oscar was up to.

As we walked into a tenement, I asked, "Is this where your connection lives?"

"Nope, not here. But before you get yourself killed, I want you to take a look at something."

I trudged after him up four flights of stairs. He pushed open a door, and we went out onto the flat roof. He led me over a few of the other flat roofs until we got to the Madison Avenue side. Then he turned to me and said, "Keep out of sight, but look down and tell me what you see."

I edged to the side of the ridge overhanging the roof. I spotted the kid, still waiting and glancing up and down the street. I saw traffic moving.

"I see the kid," I said. "He's really patient."

"Look again."

I did. But all I saw was what I had seen before—the kid, traffic, people walking. Certainly nothing unusual.

"Hey, Oscar, let's not play games," I said. "It's the same old story: the kid, cars, people walking."

"Look on the corner of One Hundred Eleventh and Madison," Oscar said. "What do you see over there?"

I peered over again. "I see a guy selling hot dogs. Nothing unusual about that."

"For crying out loud, Lefty. How many times have you seen that guy over there selling hot dogs?"

I thought about it. "I've never seen him before, but I sure have seen a lot of guys in Midtown with those carts selling hot dogs. I guess he must have lost his way and come out here."

"Stupid! I mean, you're real stupid, Lefty. Don't you know why that guy is standing there?"

"The kid or the hot-dog guy?"

"The hot-dog guy. That's another decoy cop. And you probably won't believe this, Lefty, because you're so stupid. But that kid down there isn't a kid from Jersey. He's another decoy cop."

"You're kidding!" I responded in unbelief. "That kid can't be a cop. He isn't old enough."

"That kid's a rookie."

I couldn't believe it. Within a space of three blocks I had run into three decoy cops, and I couldn't recognize one of them. But maybe Oscar was all wet. Maybe he had an over-active imagination.

"How do you know that kid's a cop?" I challenged.

"I'll tell you how. Did you notice anything when he reached into his pocket? No, you were looking at his pocket, weren't you?"

"Of course I was looking at his pocket. That's when I spotted that bulge of money."

"Well, when he reached into his pocket, I wasn't looking at his pocket. I was watching for the bulge of his gun underneath his shoulders. Sure enough, when he reached into his pants pocket, he pulled his jacket back just a little.

That's when I spotted the top of his gun. As soon as I saw that, I glanced around and spotted that guy selling hot dogs. Two things were wrong with him: one, he didn't belong in this neighborhood selling hot dogs, and two, he was staring at us. I knew we were dead ducks."

"If you knew they were cops, why didn't you take off running?"

"Lefty, you are so stupid. If we had taken off running, that rookie cop would probably have tried to be a hero and pulled his gun. They could have busted us for heaven knows what—maybe even for that chain of yours. I don't know. But let me tell you something right now, Lefty; you have to play their game. And if you know how to play it, you come out a winner."

Oscar let all that sink in. "Now there's something else you have to look for," he continued. "There are probably two other cops sitting in an unmarked car just down the street. Let's take a look."

We both crawled to where we could see over the edge of the roof and look both ways. About three blocks away I spotted a pale blue car with people sitting in it. I pointed. "What's that down there?"

Oscar strained to see, then he slapped me on the back. "You're catching on, Lefty! That's it! That's their backup car!"

"Whew, this really was another close call," I said. "So help me, if you hadn't gotten me out of there, I would have let that kid have it with my chain. And right now I'd be handcuffed and headed downtown. I hear from some of the guys on the street that they are really getting tough on muggers."

"You said it, Lefty."

We pushed back from the edge of the roof and headed toward another roof and a different exit. Oscar said the cops had probably spotted which tenement we went into and were waiting for us there.

We found an exit and started down the steps. But the cramps in my stomach were getting more and more severe. At any moment I would start vomiting. Somehow I had to get some money to buy some stuff and get off. Maybe Oscar would help me—if I made him feel sorry for me.

The pain in my stomach was strong, but not strong enough to bring anything up. So I poked a finger down my throat. That was enough. Everything came up.

The vomit splattered on the steps next to Oscar. He jumped to one side and yelled, "For crying out loud, Lefty, be careful where you're aiming!"

I made a deep gurgling sound and spit some more out. "Man," I said, "I have to get off, quick. Think you can help me?"

It's rare for one junkie to help another junkie. It doesn't happen often in the world of drug addicts. But Oscar seemed to feel a little as though I were a younger brother he needed to protect. Maybe he would have pity on me. After all, he had just saved me from prison.

"Okay, man. No problem," he said. "Come with me, and let's hope my connection has some good stuff. He almost always does. I'll give you thirty dollars of the sixty dollars. Let's hope we can get two bags each."

Good old Oscar. He saved me from jail, and now he was going to save me from getting sick. That kind of friendship was almost unheard of in the ghetto.

As we got down to the ground floor of the tenement and were about to go onto the street, Oscar motioned for me to stop. "Better let me check it out," he said. "That kid might be watching this place. Or maybe some other cops. For all I know, they may have some cop dressed like an old lady!"

I watched Oscar walk to the door, open it a crack, and peer out. I held my breath.

Then he slammed the door and jumped back. "Lefty, the streets out there are swarming with cops! There are four patrol cars. I'll bet they're waiting for us to come out. Either that kid had a radio on him and called for help or the hot-dog guy spotted us up on the roof."

"Oh, no!" I moaned. "How in the world will we get out? Oscar, if I don't get some stuff soon, I'm really going to be sick. Whatever are we going to do? How do I always manage to get myself into messes like this?"

We would have to go out onto that street sooner or later, and those cops were going to nab us both and take us away to jail. I'd had a taste of jail before, and I couldn't bear the thought of being caged up again—even overnight. And I sure didn't want my mother to find out I was on drugs. So far she didn't know. But it sure didn't look as though there were any way out this time!

2

Oscar and I waited a few more minutes, then he checked again. The cops were still swarming out there on the street. I asked him again—more desperate this time—what we were going to do.

"I'll think of something," he answered. "They're not going to send me away again."

The look on Oscar's face told the whole story. He was remembering the agony of those five years in Attica. Prison was hell!

Just then the door opened and a kid of about twelve pushed his way in. When he saw us huddled there, he got scared and took off running down to the end of the hall. Oscar took off after him.

"Mommy! Mommy! Let me in!" the kid called as he pounded nervously on the door. "Please let me in!"

I headed in that direction to see what was going on. Oscar reached into his back pocket and flicked out his switchblade. He wasn't going to stab a little kid, was he?

I heard locks click and saw the door open. The terrified kid pushed his way in. Before his mother could get the door slammed shut, Oscar was inside, too. He grabbed the startled woman and shoved the blade up under her chin. "Listen, little mother, one sound out of you, and it's all over for you and the kid. You understand?"

Oscar signaled for me to come in, telling me to shut the door behind me.

I slammed it and locked it. I looked at the woman and saw stark terror in her eyes. She had no idea what to expect from a couple of half-crazed junkies.

As Oscar forced the woman into the living room, the kid screamed. I lunged for him and slammed my hand over his mouth. His teeth sank into my flesh. I screamed and was about to let him have it with the chain I still had wrapped around my fist. But I remembered my kid brother, who was just about this kid's age. So instead of hitting him, I yelled, "You little twerp. You do that again, and I'll cut your tongue out!"

That scared him into quietness.

"Now, ma'am, nobody will get hurt if you just do what my buddy and I say," Oscar told the woman. "All we're going to do is spend about an hour here in your apartment. And nobody will get hurt if you cooperate. You understand?"

He punctuated his sentences by jabbing his switchblade lightly into her chin. Poor woman. Her face was white as a sheet, and her eyes bugged out. She didn't know whether we were going to mug her or rape her or what. I really felt sorry for her.

Oscar moved her over and sat her down on the sofa, saying, "Now, little mother, I'm going to pull this switchblade away from your chin. But it will be right here, handy. You're going to sit right there, and I'm going to sit here next to you. And nobody needs to get hurt. Understand?"

She was so scared that she couldn't even move her lips, much less say anything.

What was Oscar up to? Why were we going to stay here an hour? I kept thinking that I didn't have an hour. I needed to get off right away. I was getting sicker by the minute.

The kid was whimpering over by his mother's feet, close enough so Oscar could keep an eye on both of them. I dropped into a nearby chair and tried to relax. But my stomach was churning, and before I knew what was happening, I had vomited all over the floor. "Excuse me, ma'am," I said, half-embarrassed. "I really didn't mean to do that."

She pointed toward the bathroom, too frightened to say anything.

I headed down the little hallway, and my stomach started churning again. This time I was able to make it to the toilet.

I felt a little better in a few minutes. I even got some toilet paper and cleaned up the mess I'd made. I wasn't worried about the woman's apartment, but the stuff smelled so bad that I was afraid it would make me sick again just to smell it.

I looked at the clock. Half-past three. We'd been there

about half an hour. We'd be leaving at four. But why four o'clock?

I eased back into a chair and studied the woman. She was rather attractive—a little younger than my mother. I wondered where her husband was—or whether she had a husband. She certainly didn't volunteer any information, and I didn't dare ask any questions. I was concentrating on how to keep from being sicker. I knew there was only one way to get over this. I had to get off.

Oscar looked at the clock and announced, "Just fifteen more minutes." I couldn't imagine what was going to happen at four.

The minutes ticked by so slowly. Then at four Oscar said, "Okay, everything ought to be clear."

I wanted to ask how he knew, but I decided it would be best to keep my mouth shut. Oscar had gotten me out of those problems with the decoy cops, so I felt I could trust him.

"Go on down and take a look out the front door," he said to me. "See if the way is clear."

"What? You want me to go out there with all those cops?"

"Don't worry; they'll be gone."

How could he be so positive?

I got up, unlocked the apartment door, and walked to the end of the hall. Then I opened the tenement door and checked the street. No cops. I looked the other way. No cops! That was the strangest thing I had ever experienced. But how did Oscar know?

I ran back to the apartment. "Oscar, you rascal, all the cops are gone!" I announced.

He smiled knowingly.

Then his face got serious as he turned to the woman. "Little mother, I want you to get something straight, and I do mean straight," he said menacingly. "You don't tell a soul about this little visit. You don't tell a person about this knife held at your throat. I'll tell you something. If I find out you said anything to anyone about our being here, I'll come back and get you, and get you good. I'll rob everything you got in this place. After I get through with that, I'll cut you all up. Your pretty little face will be scarred for the rest of your life. And your little boy here—you may never see him alive again! You understand what I'm telling you?"

The woman nodded nervously. So did the kid. These poor people had probably been the victims of muggers before—probably junkies like us.

As Oscar grabbed the door handle, he snarled, "Listen, little mother, we're mean, terrible junkies. We're the meanest junkies in all of New York City. We don't stop at anything! So one word out of you, and it's all over." He motioned with his finger across his throat.

Both the woman and the boy nodded. I knew they weren't about to open their mouths to anybody.

When we got to the front door of the tenement, Oscar just boldly marched out. I held back a little, just in case the cops opened fire from some hiding place.

When nothing happened, I followed him out to the sidewalk. No cops. Nothing.

"Okay, Oscar, let's not play any more games. How did you know that at four o'clock there wouldn't be any cops out here on the street? You had inside information."

"No—brains, man, brains! I've been watching and noticed that they change shifts in the precinct at four o'clock. That means that all the cops on the street go in. And those coming on duty haven't gotten their assignments yet. So at four o'clock they're all down at the police station."

So that was it! Man, Oscar was smart. But why was he a junkie if he were so smart? It didn't seem to me that anybody with any brains would let himself get hooked. But, who was I to criticize? I had always bragged I'd never get hooked—I could take the stuff or leave it. But I couldn't leave it now. I had to have it. And I had to have it now!

"Who's your connection?" I asked as we headed toward 112th Street.

"Ever hear of Spino?"

"Spino? Sure have! Man, he's big time! I didn't know that's who you bought your drugs from."

"Well, Lefty, it's this way. The junk they're selling on the street can really be dangerous. Man, some of that stuff has poison in it. Either that, or it's nothing but milk sugar and quinine. No heroin whatever. And when I pay good money for it, I want good stuff."

I knew what Oscar was getting at. Every so often someone in the neighborhood died of an overdose. It wasn't that the stuff was really good, but it was a "hot shot." It was fatal.

"There is one thing for sure," Oscar went on. "I've always been able to trust Spino. He's never ripped me off."

"I wish I could say that about my connection. I buy from Luigi Domino."

Oscar laughed. "Domino? How come you get your stuff from him? He's nothing but a two-bit operator. Everybody knows he doesn't have really good stuff."

"I guess I've stayed with him because I started with him. He's the one who turned me on to drugs. So I just kept going back to him. Habit, I guess. But, man, I wish I had a connection like Spino. But he deals only with certain customers. Right?"

"Right," Oscar replied. "He's got a few special customers. He told me that one time he got busted for selling to an undercover cop. After that, he decided to do two things. First, he would always have the best stuff in the neighborhood. Second, he would select his customers—not the other way around.

"I used to buy from him before I got sent up, so he's been in business for more than five years. He must be making a mint! I saw him tooling around in a new Cadillac the other day. And you should see all the girls he sports around town with."

Oscar was drooling with envy.

"Are you sure he's not a pimp, too?"

"Spino, a pimp? No way. He doesn't have to pimp any girls. He's making it off us junkies. But maybe we'll see some of his girls when we go to his apartment. He's not out on the streets this time of the afternoon, but I know where he lives. I've never been to his apartment. But they tell me he's got an apartment full of luscious girls!"

Any other time that would have really excited me. But right now my mind was only on my stomach. I was so sick; I had to get off.

A few minutes' walk brought us to the apartment house where Spino lived. It didn't look too bad.

We headed up the stairs. A guy was coming down the stairs. He mumbled hello, but I didn't respond. I was still thinking about one thing: drugs. In a few minutes my misery would be over. I would ascend to the highest heaven and forget about the hell I lived in. And I knew I was going to get good stuff because Oscar had said Spino had the best.

When I became aware of a shuffling right behind me, I whirled around quickly. I wasn't quite prepared for what I saw: Oscar with his gun at that guy's head!

Now what was up? Another plainclothes cop?

I started back down the steps, but Oscar yelled, "Wait, Lefty! Come here a minute."

I obediently trotted back to where Oscar stood with one arm around the guy's neck and his gun at the guy's temple.

"Please don't hurt me!" the guy begged. "Please don't hurt me!"

"Shut up!" Oscar yelled, "or I'll splatter your brains against that wall!"

When the guy quieted, Oscar said to me, "Lefty, I want you to meet a dirty, rotten swindler. This dude's a dirty crook, and we're going to fix him."

Didn't Oscar know the laws of the jungle? One crook was never supposed to mug another crook.

"This scum goes to see people who get welfare checks," Oscar went on. "He acts as though he's really doing them a favor by cashing their checks for them. But then he sells them insurance they don't need—death-benefit insurance. My poor grandmother has to pay fifty bucks a month to this scum. And it won't do her a bit of good. When she dies, her relatives will fight over the money."

The poor guy's eyes bugged out. I guess he must have thought the end of the world had come for him.

I heard a click as Oscar cocked his gun. "Oscar! Oscar!" I yelled. "Hold on! Don't pull that trigger!"

I sure didn't want to be an accomplice to a murder! Besides, if I got busted now before I got off, they'd throw me in a cell, and I'd have to kick my habit cold turkey. I knew the agony of that would be unbearable.

"Please! Please!" the man begged. "I have a wife and three kids at home. Please think about them. Have mercy! Please!"

Oscar jabbed the revolver deeper into the man's temple. "Shut up, I told you!" he yelled. "Or the next time your wife and three kids see you, you'll be in a casket, with your head blown off!"

Oscar turned to me. "Reach into his pockets," he said, "we'll take everything he's got."

I ran my hand into one back pocket. Nothing. I checked

the other one. Nothing. When I checked the front ones, all I found were three quarters.

Oscar cussed. "Where's your money?" he demanded.

"Don't hurt me! Don't hurt me!" the man begged. Then he dropped his hand toward his belt and began to unbuckle it.

"Oh, no, you don't!" Oscar screamed. "Keep your hands up in the air!"

"Let me take off my belt," the guy responded. "I've got something to show you."

"Check him out," Oscar told me. "Be sure he doesn't have a gun or knife on him."

I patted the guy's hips and ran my hands down his legs, then up around his arms. Nothing. But I thought I felt something around his midsection. I ran my hands along there again. Something was creating a bulge.

"He's got something here along his waistline," I told Oscar.

"That's what I was reaching for," the man said. "Here, let me show you."

As he dropped his hands again, Oscar jabbed the gun and yelled, "Nothing doing! You keep those hands up!"

I undid the belt and pulled it out of the loops. Then I realized what we had—a money belt!

Quickly I unzipped it. Stashed inside were fives and tens and twenties. Wow! There must be a bundle here!

Oscar's eyes widened. "Now that's more like it!" he said. "And I want to tell you something, mister. This isn't any holdup. I'm just pulling a little Robin Hood. I'm going to take this money and give it to the poor. And so help me, if you go squealing to the cops, the next time I catch you, I'll blast your brains all over the wall—no questions asked. You understand what I'm saying?"

The man quivered. "Please don't hurt me! Please don't hurt me!" he begged. "I mean, I didn't mean to do anybody any harm. Don't hurt me!"

"I ought to kill scum like you," Oscar responded. "I ought to kill you dead."

"Oh, mister, I won't breathe a word about this to anybody," the man said. "I won't breathe one word."

With that he pushed off his pants and his shoes and kicked them down the stairs. He took off his shirt and threw that down the stairs, too. Then he walked over and sat in a corner.

"What do you think you're doing?" Oscar demanded.

"I just wanted to let you know I'm not going to follow you anywhere," he answered.

Oscar grinned. "That's more like it," he said. "You'd better believe you're not going to follow us. And you're not going to say one word to the cops, are you?"

The man shook his head. He was too scared to try anything.

Oscar fished the money out of the belt and stuffed it into his pocket. I wondered whether he would split it with me.

We took a few more steps up the stairs, and Oscar turned. "Mister, my friend and I have a little business to do up here. In a few minutes we'll be back down. You're going to sit right there until we come back and I tell you you can get up. You understand?"

The guy was willing to do anything Oscar said. He pulled his knees up under his chin and threw his arms around his legs. "I'm not going to move an inch from here until you tell me it's okay," he said. "Go do your business. I'll still be here."

It was a little chilly in the stairway, and the guy's arms and legs were shaking so much he could hardly control himself. He looked as though any minute he might pass out from fright.

But what did I care? Oscar and I had what we wanted: money! And we were on our way to Spino's place to buy some drugs. I could see the light at the end of the tunnel.

But I had no idea what else was in that tunnel!

3

Oscar and I finally got to third floor of the apartment building and walked to the end of the hall. Oscar knocked lightly.

For a quick moment I had forgotten my sickness. But now it returned. The pain hit the pit of my stomach, and I bent over. Oscar grabbed me by the shirt collar and lifted me up. "Stay cool, man," he said. "You'll be okay in a couple of minutes."

Oscar knocked again. Still no answer. Oh, no! What if Spino had gone somewhere? Maybe he was out on the street pushing drugs. No, he *had* to be here!

This time Oscar banged on the door. Then the door opened just a crack.

I heard a voice boom out, "Oscar Rodriguez, you good-for-nothing junkie; what are you doing here?"

I jumped back. This wasn't the kind of reception I expected from a big-time pusher like Spino!

Then the door flew open, and Spino and two other huge guys grabbed us and jerked us into the apartment. I felt myself being thrown up against a wall. The next thing I knew I had one guy's switchblade poking at my chin.

I glanced over and saw that the other guy had Oscar in the same position. They sure were ready for us!

Then I glanced at Spino. We should have known that a big-time operator would have bodyguards. But why was he treating us this way? We didn't mean any harm. All we wanted to do was to buy from him.

Spino was right in front of Oscar's face, screaming, "You dirty junkie! What are you doing here?"

Because of the tip of a switchblade sticking in his chin, Oscar answered rather meekly, "Hey, man, no big deal. I just came up to get a buy, that's all."

"Okay, Oscar, I know you. But who is this other jerk?"

Any other time, if somebody had called me a jerk, he would have felt my anger. But I couldn't do anything about it at the moment.

"That's my friend Lefty," Oscar answered in measured tones. "He came to buy, too."

Without warning, Spino backhanded Oscar. "How many times do I have to tell guys like you how it is with me?" he demanded. "You know, Oscar, that I select my own customers. How many times do I have to say it to get this through that thick skull of yours? You don't bring customers to me. I find my own customers." Then he looked in my direction. "You say this guy's name is Lefty? He could be an undercover cop."

"For crying out loud, Spino," Oscar answered, "you know better than that. Just pull up his sleeve. That will be your answer. Lefty's no cop."

The big, burly guy who had me kept the knife under my throat with one hand, but with the other he jerked up my sleeve. I threw my arm out for him to look at the track at my armpits.

"Okay, Mike," Spino said, "he looks okay."

Mike jerked his blade away from my chin, and I drew a deep sigh of relief.

Spino slowly moved in front of me. "What's your name, kid?"

"Lefty Taggart."

He slapped me across the face. Oh, did it sting! I bristled.

"Spino, don't hit Lefty!" Oscar shouted. "That's his real name. Honest."

"I don't care about his name," Spino answered. "I just wanted to teach this young punk a lesson. That smack across the face was for coming here to my apartment. I guarantee that if either of you shows up here again, you won't get just a slap in the face. I'll turn my boys loose and let them stab you forty-six times each. I mean, they'll have free reign to mutilate these bodies of yours. Do you understand?"

We both nodded. You just didn't cross up a pusher. These boys meant business. They *would* kill you.

"Spino, we're sorry," Oscar said. "We won't come up here again. But since we're here, can I get four bags?"

I held my breath. He just had to say yes.

"Yeah, man," Spino answered. "You can have four bags. How much money do you have on you?"

I guess Oscar must have really been shook up over the turn of events, because he pulled out every penny he had—the sixty dollars he had taken from the decoy cop and the money he had pulled out of the guy's money belt on the stairs. He had just over three hundred dollars! That meant that instead of four bags, we could probably get twenty!

"I guess I had a little more money than what I thought," Oscar said sheepishly. "Maybe we could buy more than four bags?"

Spino laughed—a deep, hollow laugh. "Tell you what,

Oscar. The price just went up. I mean, just as you came in the door, I got word that drugs went up. I mean, way up."

I didn't like the way he said it.

"What are you talking about?" Oscar asked.

"Oscar, I have to teach you a lesson. You made a bad mistake when you came up here, so you have to learn a lesson. Grab his money, boys."

Before Oscar knew what was happening, those two brutes had snatched all the money out of his hands. His hand went toward his .45 automatic pistol. But that's as far as he got. One of the brutes anticipated that movement, knocked Oscar's feet out from under him, and sent him sprawling across the floor. In a millionth of a second, that brute was on Oscar and had jerked the pistol from Oscar's belt.

"Hey, wait a minute!" Oscar yelled. "Spino, you know I'd never pull a gun on you."

Spino laughed again. "Yeah, I know, Oscar. I mean, like you never would want to hurt anybody, would you? You just like the feel of that gun in your belt."

Then Spino spit in disgust. "Don't give me any of your nonsense, Oscar. You'd do anything you thought you could get by with. You're nothing but a dirty, filthy junkie!"

I was totally unprepared for this turn of events. They had taken our money. Now were they going to kill us? I wasn't going to stand still for that. I'd better do something while I had a chance. But what? The only thing I had on me was my switchblade. I'd dropped my chain when I got sick back in the woman's apartment and had forgotten to pick it up again.

As soon as I thought of my switchblade, I must have instinctively started to reach for it, because the next thing I knew, the other guy had me pinned to the wall—and he had my switchblade out in a moment's time.

Now it really looked as though this were the end for Oscar and me. No guns, no switchblades—and facing two monsters who had probably killed before, and who wouldn't mind doing it again.

"Oscar, get up off the floor," Spino ordered.

Oscar got up slowly, somewhat confused by it all.

"Oscar, you've been a good customer of mine," Spino started. "But Big Daddy's got to teach his little boy a lesson. So for your three hundred bucks, I'll sell you four bags."

"Spino," Oscar begged, "don't rip me off that way, man! You're more decent than that!"

Spino laughed that sinister laugh again. It almost made me vomit.

"Man, I'm doing you a favor," Spino responded. "The last guy who messed me up will never be found. I mean, man, they're still looking for his body, but they'll never find it."

He laughed again.

My heart was beating like crazy. Somehow we had to get out of this, and Oscar sure wasn't helping things any. I'd be satisfied to get four bags and get out alive.

"As I say, Oscar," Spino said, "I have to teach you not to come up here." Then he turned to his bodyguards. "Keep an eye on them while I'm gone."

A few minutes later, Spino returned with four bags, which he tossed at Oscar. Then he looked over at me.

"Where are we now, Lefty?" he asked.

What did he mean? We were at 112th Street. So I blurted out the address.

No sooner were the words out of my mouth than Spino slapped me again. "Lefty," he yelled as he stuck his face right into mine, "you don't know this address. Do you hear me?"

I nodded. Dumb me. I'd better think a little sharper. So I blurted out, "I mean, this is seven-thirty-two West Sixth Street. Right?"

"Don't get smart, kid," Spino warned. "If anybody asks you where you've been, you just tell them you don't know. And let me make something else clear. If you ever come here again, or tell anybody else about my being here, I'll send my boys out after you. They have switchblades that look three feet long, and they'll cut you up into little pieces and feed you to the pigeons in Central Park. You got that?"

I nodded nervously. I wasn't about to say anything to provoke Spino or his boys.

"Okay, give them back their weapons," Spino said to his bodyguards. "I think they've learned their lesson. They won't try anything."

One guy handed me my switchblade, and I stuffed it back into my pocket. They gave Oscar his revolver. Then they pushed us out into the hallway and slammed the door behind us.

We hurried down the steps. Sure enough, there was that poor man still huddled in the corner. Not only was he still trembling, but now he was crying.

"I'm glad you are going to give that money back to the poor," the man whimpered. "I've been sitting here thinking about it, and I say it's mighty nice of you, mister. Besides—"

"Shut up!" Oscar ordered. I guess he must have been thinking what crossed my mind at that point. The money we had stolen had in turn been stolen from us!

Back outside, we headed toward 110th and Madison. "Do you have any works on you?" I asked Oscar.

"Yeah," he said. "I have my works taped to my leg. Why?"

"I mean, man, I'm sick. I need to get off right now. Why don't we duck into one of these tenements and get off?"

"Wait just a minute," Oscar replied. "There's no way that I'm going to let you use my works unless you give me ten bucks."

"Ten dollars?" I screamed. "You know I don't have a dime on me!"

"As I said, ten bucks," Oscar repeated. "I charge everybody the same."

"Oscar, I'm so sick. Have pity. My works are up in the apartment, but my old lady is there. You know I can't get off with her there. Besides, my kid brother's at home, too. There's no way I can get off up there and get by with it."

"Sorry, Lefty, but you wouldn't want to use my works, anyway. You see, I have hepatitis. If you use my works, you'll get stuck with a dirty needle and get hepatitis, too. You might even die!"

I grabbed him by the shoulders and looked straight into his eyes. "Oscar," I yelled, "you're lying! You don't have hepatitis. I can tell by your eyes! Come on. I'll pay you the ten bucks later."

"Listen, Lefty, my chances of getting ten bucks from you later are pretty remote," Oscar answered. "But I want to tell you something. There's absolutely no way I loan my works to anybody. And, man, I think you ought to look at your own eyes. I think *you've* got hepatitis!" He pushed me away.

"Here," he said. He held out two bags of heroin. "Take them and go. They're yours."

I snatched them from his hand and took off running. "Have it your way," I called back. "I have to take a chance with my old lady and kid brother."

I was out of breath by the time I arrived at our tenement house, and I still had to get to the fourth floor. It made me mad again. Why did we poor people have to live on the fourth floor? Why couldn't we afford to live on a lower floor?

Anyway, I was barely navigating by the time I pushed open the door to our apartment and headed for the bedroom.

"Who's there?" Mom called.

"Lefty," I yelled back.

I pushed up my mattress to get my works. I had slit a place in it where I could hide them. Then I headed for the bathroom. "Lefty, what's the matter with you?" Mom called. "Come in here."

I didn't answer. I was about to pass out from the pain.

Quickly I unraveled the stocking, put it around my arm, twisted it, and began to pump my veins.

Almost now. . . . Here's hoping I hit a vein. I drilled. Oh, no! I missed. Jerking the needle out I pumped my hands again to swell the veins. Then I slowly pushed the needle in and squeezed.

That beautiful solution started into my veins. I waited for the high. This was what I lived for.

Then it happened. I felt my body falling into space. Only it wasn't a high. Had I gotten some bad drugs? Was I dying from a "hot shot"?

Then I realized what must have happened. That dirty Spino must have decided we'd be better off dead because we knew where he lived. But he didn't want to kill us at his apartment and then have to dispose of our bodies. So he just fixed up that heroin. He had put something in that drug to kill us. I had to warn Oscar. I started toward the door, and everything began falling in on me.

The next thing I knew, I realized I was staring up into

my mother's face. "Lefty! Lefty!" she was screaming. "Can you hear me? Can you hear me?"

I blinked my eyes. No, I wasn't dead. I guess I had over-dosed. Spino must have sold us good stuff—it was just too much for my body to take all at once. I wasn't used to that quality.

I tried to get up, but my body was numb; I could scarcely move. Mother saw what I was trying to do and helped me onto the toilet.

My vision cleared, and I noticed the needle was still stuck in my arm. Blood was oozing out. It looked horrible.

Mother grabbed a washcloth, soaked it, and started wiping off the blood.

Then Nicky appeared in the doorway. "What's the matter, Lefty?" he wanted to know. "We thought you died!"

"Keep still, Nicky," Mother said. "Your brother is in terrible trouble."

I wondered whether Nicky understood that his brother was a junkie.

He came into the bathroom and spotted the needle in the sink. "What's this?" he demanded.

Mother snatched the needle out of his hand and slammed it into the wall. I cringed as I heard it snap. Then she threw the syringe to the floor and stomped it into little pieces. I had never seen her so angry. But I sat there un-moved. I didn't care what happened. Besides, I could al-ways get another needle.

"He's on drugs, isn't he?" Nicky demanded. "I've seen things like this on television."

"Shut up!" Mom screamed. "I don't ever want anyone to mention drugs in this house again!"

Nicky started to say something else, but Mom reached up to backhand him across the mouth. I grabbed her arm, but it made me lose my balance, and I toppled off the toilet, striking my head as I fell. I expected to be knocked out or to feel pain, but I felt nothing. The heroin was still working in my body.

When Mother was distracted because of my falling, Nicky raised his fist toward her. "Nicky, don't do it!" I yelled.

That warned her, and she wheeled around to see his raised fist. She cuffed him a good one and sent him sprawling out of the bathroom into the hall. My mother was only five feet tall, but she knew how to hit!

Nicky started crying. Then he screamed in defiance, "I'm going to be a junkie, too! I'm going to be a junkie, too!"

Mom grabbed a towel, folded it in half, and started toward Nicky. "Ma! Ma!" I yelled. "Don't do it! Don't do it! That won't stop him!"

My words brought her back to her senses. She wheeled around and looked down on me. "Lefty, never in my whole life would I have ever believed that something like this would happen in our family. You know that your father was murdered out there on the street, the victim of a mugger. But, Lefty, I never told you that the young punk who killed your father was a junkie. That kid is in the penitentiary for his crime. But he took something away from me that nothing in all this world can ever replace. He took your father from me. When I found out that kid was a junkie, I swore I would never have anything to do with junkies. Ever! And I meant it. And now I find out I have a junkie here in my house. But not for long!"

She leaned over, grabbed me by the hair, and dragged me out into the hall.

"Stop! Stop!" I yelled. "You must be out of your mind!"

I managed to stumble to my feet, but she still held me by the hair and forced me down the hall to the apartment door and pushed me out into the hallway. I was still weak from the overdose, and my body couldn't stop before hitting the wall. I glanced off it and slumped to the floor.

I just lay there for a moment or two, wondering what this was all about. The door opened again, and Mother started throwing my clothes out at me.

"Lefty," she screamed, "don't ever darken this door again! You junkies are all the same. I don't know how many people you've mugged or what you've done to support your habit. But I do know this. No junkie will ever live in my house. You'll live on the streets now until you kick that habit. When you're clean, you can come back. But not before!"

Was this really happening? Or was it a hallucination from the overdose? All I could see were more clothes flying out the door and landing all over the hall.

I was too weak to protest or to try to force my way back in. So I just lay there, half-propped up by the wall, and wondering what to do next.

Then our apartment door opened again. Nicky pushed past my mother and grabbed my clothes, throwing them back inside the apartment. Mother backhanded him and shouted, "You get inside, this minute! And let this be a lesson to you. No one, and I mean no one, who takes drugs will ever darken the door of this apartment. Now take a good look at your brother. He's a good-for-nothing junkie, just like the good-for-nothing junkie who murdered your father. He's a filthy junkie. He's not fit to live with decent human beings!"

I knew I was in a stupor, but that didn't lessen the shock I felt. No one had ever told me my dad had been killed by a junkie. Would it have made a difference if I had known that? Would it have kept me away from drugs?

Those questions really didn't matter much now. I was hooked. I was a junkie.

Mom grabbed Nicky by the back of his shirt, jerked him back into the apartment, and slammed the door. Then I heard the lock click.

I stared at the closed door. Part of me wanted to cry and tell my mother I was sorry. Part of me wanted to tear down that door and smack my mother across the room and show her she couldn't treat me this way. But somehow I couldn't do that. I felt guilty about disappointing her. She had always wanted me to grow up to be someone she could be proud of. Life had been so cruel to her. And now this.

I finally eased my weakened body up and looked down at the pile of clothes at my feet. Then I started to think about myself. What was I going to do? Where was I going to go? Who wanted a junkie?

4

My clothes lying there in the hall seemed to mock me. They were all I had left now. Mother had said I couldn't come back to this apartment. But where could I go?

I flattened out one shirt and piled all the other clothes in it. Then I rolled it up, tied the arms together, picked up the bundle, and headed for the street.

Maybe Oscar could tell me what to do. He always seemed to have a lot of answers.

I knew Oscar lived somewhere nearby. Funny thing: He never told me anything about his place, and I really wasn't sure where it was. I hoped his mother wasn't like mine. Maybe she'd be kind to me and take me in.

When I got to the area where I thought Oscar lived, I looked around. Then it hit me. Who could I ask about

Oscar Rodriguez? New York City is awfully big. Lots of people don't even know the names of the people who live in the next apartment!

"Hey, good looking, want to have a good time?" a voice behind me purred. I turned around to see a very attractive girl. But I knew what she was up to. She was a prostitute.

The wheels started turning, and I decided to have a little fun—only not the kind she had in mind.

"I'm sorry, sister, but you just propositioned the wrong person," I said. "I'm a detective from the police department, and I'm taking you in for prostitution. I see my disguise worked."

Her mouth flew open, and her eyes bugged out. "No! No! Please don't, officer," she pleaded. "I didn't mean that the way it sounded."

I grabbed her by the arm. "What's your name, young lady?"

She started to tremble all over. I looked down and noticed she had a track. She'd been around for quite a while, shooting drugs.

Then she started to cry.

"I said, 'What's your name?' " I repeated.

"Karen Godwick," she said between sobs.

"Karen Godwick? Haven't you been busted before for prostitution?"

"Oh, no! No! I'm no prostitute. I'm just a girl out here on the street looking for a boyfriend. And you looked so young and handsome—and kind of lonely, too. You know what I mean?"

This was so much fun I decided to string her along a little longer.

"Now don't give me any stories like that, lady," I said. "I'm taking you in. Now!"

"Listen, officer," she sobbed, "I had no idea you were a

cop—I mean, a policeman. I know the cops are using disguises, but you don't look over eighteen. And when I saw you with that bundle of clothes. . . . Oh, you know how it is. I just thought you seemed so lonesome, and I wanted to cheer you up a little. Please let me go. Please don't bust me this time. I promise I will never say anything like that again in my whole life."

I couldn't keep a straight face any longer and started to laugh.

"What's the matter?" she demanded. "Why are you laughing?"

"Karen," I finally sputtered, "I'm no police officer. The name's Lefty Taggart, and I'm just looking for a place to stay."

"What?" she yelled. "You were just stringing me along?"

I nodded and then doubled over with laughter.

But Karen was furious, and told me so in no uncertain terms.

I finally straightened up enough that I regained my composure and turned to walk away. That's when I felt her hand grab the back of my collar and spin me around. There she stood, feet apart—with her switchblade aimed right at my heart!

"Listen, Lefty Taggart, I don't mind playing games, but don't you ever play that game on me again!" she yelled. "I just finished doing six months, and I'm not about to go back in."

I could tell she was deadly serious, and I sure wasn't laughing now. "Karen, stay cool, will you?" I said. "I didn't mean any harm. You see, my old lady just threw me out of the house because she found out I'm a junkie. I have to find a place to stay. That's the reason for this bundle of clothes. I guess I was just looking for something to take my mind off my problems. I shouldn't have treated you that way. I'm sorry."

She dropped her arm, folded the switchblade, and tucked it back inside her blouse.

"Whew!" I said. "That's better. Now, let me ask you something. I'm looking for a friend of mine, Oscar Rodriguez. Do you know him?"

"Oscar Rodriguez? Yes, I know him."

"Do you know where he lives?"

"Sure. Just up the block there," Karen said as she pointed. "It's the light brown tenement. He lives in the basement."

"Thanks, Karen. See you around."

"Hey, wait, Lefty. Do you really know Oscar personally?"

"Yes. Why?"

"Man, are you lucky! You should see his apartment. I mean, that guy has one of the plushest apartments in New York City! It doesn't look like much on the outside, but inside he's got all kinds of plush furniture, thick carpet, piped-in stereo, three huge TV sets. I mean, man, that is a *gorgeous* place!"

Could this be the same Oscar I knew? Why would he have a place like that? He must have some game on the side, because no junkie could be living in luxury like that!

When I looked at Karen quizzically, she continued, "You see, I used to live with Oscar, but one day he threw me out on the street. I sure wish I lived there now. I mean, it's out of this world—like heaven!"

Without even a good-bye to Karen, I hurried to the light brown apartment building, hoping against hope that Oscar would take me in. Anything would be better than the street. But to have three TV sets and stereo and thick carpeting.

Wow! This was almost too good to be true.

In no time I reached the tenement Karen had pointed out. From the outside it did look like all the others—worn and beaten.

There was only one apartment in the basement, and the outside door looked as though it hadn't been painted in years. But inside, from what Karen had told me, heaven awaited!

I knocked. No answer. Again. Still no answer.

The doorknob turned when I touched it, so I opened the door. When I stepped inside, I wasn't prepared for what I found. It was the dirtiest, filthiest basement tenement I had ever seen—and I had seen a lot of them. Banana peelings, empty cans, even rotten tomatoes and all kinds of other garbage were strewn all over the place. Over in one corner I spotted a filthy mattress. The table was a couple of stained apple boxes with a candle on one of them. In what must have once been a kitchen, the cupboard door had been broken off, and there was filth everywhere.

That Karen! Either she had lied to me to get the last laugh or I had come to the wrong apartment.

As I was picking my way through the garbage, I heard footsteps behind me. I whirled around. Standing at the door was Oscar.

"Is this where you live?" I asked.

"Yes," he said, hanging his head a little. "It isn't much, but it beats sleeping on the sidewalk."

I wasn't sure I agreed with him. I thought of my mother's apartment. It wasn't much, but compared to this, it was a paradise!

Oscar spotted the bundle of clothes. "Hey, man," he said, "what's the matter? Looks like you're hoofing it."

"Yes. My old lady found out I'm a junkie and threw me out. I have no place to go."

"Sounds familiar," Oscar grunted. "When I got sent up the river five years ago, my old man and old lady told me they never wanted to see me again. So ever since then I've been on my own. When I got out of prison, I slept at every place you could imagine—subway stations, burned-out tenements. I even used to sleep at Grand Central Station in the winter because it was warm there. But this is where I am now. As I say, it beats the streets."

I didn't know whether I wanted to stay here or not. Should I ask?

I didn't have to. "Hey, man, throw your clothes over there in the corner," Oscar continued. "And you won't have somebody nagging you about keeping the place clean. It would take ten years to clean it up, so I never bother. But at least you'll have a place to lay your head at night."

I realized that it was better than nothing and rationalized that I could keep a lookout for something better. Besides, it was already pretty late, and I didn't have a penny to my name.

We talked awhile and eventually went to sleep. I guess we didn't wake up until noon. Oscar scrounged a little food together and then announced, "Lefty, I'm headed down to Fourteenth Street. There's a guy down there who pays me good money for some quick work. You want to join me?"

"Man, I don't want to work my first day away from home," I protested. "I mean, I don't want to get hooked with a steady job or anything."

Oscar laughed. "No, I'm not talking about a steady job. I called the guy yesterday about this. Come on. Each of us can make a hundred bucks in an hour or so."

"Doing what?"

"Listen, I'd better not tell you now. I mean, if I told you now what we were going to do, you might run off and do it yourself without me. You'd make all the money. No, I don't tell anybody what I'm doing. The only way you'll know is if you come along with me."

I decided I sure didn't have anything to lose by going along. I wasn't about to spend the day in this mess. And I had to get some money to get off again.

As soon as I thought of drugs, I remembered what had happened. "Oscar, I got off yesterday with those two bags we got from Spino," I said, "and I overdosed."

"I should have warned you, Lefty. Watch the stuff that Spino sells you. I mean, he's got good stuff. This stuff you get from the guys off the street is nothing. But when you load up with Spino's stuff, you can't get greedy."

"Do I ever know! I'll tell you, I really thought I had gotten a 'hot shot.' I even wondered whether he might have put something in that stuff to kill us!"

"No. Spino may be kind of mean at times, but he's never been known to give anybody a 'hot shot' or anything like that. He's just got good stuff, that's all."

Oscar picked up a small crowbar from among the trash on the floor. "Hey, man," I said, "are you going to break into somebody's apartment?"

"Not today. But I'll need this. We can make some quick money on this job, and we won't have to take anything to a fence, either."

With that, Oscar headed out the door, and I trailed after him. He pushed the crowbar into the side of his pants along his leg. Then he pulled his shirt over the top.

"We'd better take the subway," he said. "It's a long way to walk to Fourteenth Street."

I started to protest that I didn't have a dime to my name and turned my pockets inside out to prove it. That's when I found those three quarters. I had forgotten that when I found them on that creep we had robbed yesterday, I had stuck them in my pocket. At the time I had been disgusted that that was all I found on the guy. Now they were a life-saver!

Down on Fourteenth Street we walked along the street in front of a lot of small shops. Oscar turned and went inside one that sold jeans and tennis shoes.

Evidently the owner recognized Oscar because he immediately motioned us into a back office, where he joined us.

In a hushed, confidential tone he told us, "The truck should be on the block about three. It will be a red truck. On its side will be BOONE'S DELIVERY SERVICE, so you shouldn't have any trouble recognizing it."

Oscar stood there nodding. So help me, I didn't know what was up, but I also knew that this was no time to ask questions. So I just stood there and nodded, too—as though I knew what was happening.

"Okay, here's my deal," the man continued. "A hundred bucks a case."

"A hundred bucks?" Oscar yelled. The man nervously shushed him, and Oscar continued in low tones, "Man, you have to give me more than that! I mean, this is risky business."

Risky business? Now I was really getting nervous.

"Listen, Oscar," the man said, "you think it's risky? It's not nearly as risky for you as it is for me. You do your thing and disappear. Me? I have to stay here. In fact, the other day the cops were in here asking a whole bunch of questions. I'm getting pretty nervous about this deal myself, and I may have to shut it off for a while. So this is it. It's a hundred bucks, or no deal."

"Well," Oscar said, "since you've been a good customer, I'll do it once more for a hundred bucks. But no more. Next time the price goes up to one hundred twenty-five dollars."

The man didn't respond, and Oscar turned and headed out of the store, with me still following.

Farther down Fourteenth Street we spotted the red delivery truck, just as the man had said.

"First, we stand here for a few minutes and check out this guy's deliveries," Oscar explained.

We both leaned against a nearby building, trying to look nonchalant. We watched as a delivery man put two cases on a hand truck, locked the doors of the delivery truck, and then wheeled the boxes inside a nearby store.

As soon as he got inside, Oscar said, "Okay, quick now!"

We dashed to the back of the truck. "Get real close," Oscar instructed, "as though you're unlocking this lock. No, real close to me. That's right. Now bend over so nobody can see what I'm doing."

As I obeyed, Oscar whipped out his crowbar and pried. The lock broke open. He pulled the door, jumped up inside, scanned the boxes, grabbed one, and pushed it to me. Then he grabbed another one, jumped out of the truck, and started carrying it down the street. "Follow me," he called. "Hurry—but don't go too fast. We're just delivery men."

I was beginning to catch on now—especially since I had noticed that the boxes were labeled TENNIS SHOES.

We walked briskly—as fast as we could under the circumstances. The boxes were bulky, and they were heavy—almost too heavy.

"Just pretend you're making deliveries," Oscar whispered back to me. "Look innocent." But I noticed he kept glancing back toward the red delivery truck—and walking faster!

As nervous as I was, it sure was hard to look innocent. I expected that at any moment a cop would grab me by the shoulder. And where can you hide a case of tennis shoes? I was also afraid the truck driver would come out and spot us and yell, "Thief! Thief!"

But we soon got lost in the crush of people. No way could that driver spot us now. So we kept elbowing our way through the crowds until we finally got back to the shoe store.

Oscar walked right in the front door, yelling, "Delivery! Delivery! Excuse me, folks. Delivery!"

I took the cue and mumbled the same thing.

The manager met us at the back of the store and pointed to where we could put the boxes down. Was I glad! My arms were killing me!

"Hello there, Mr. Lozinski," Oscar said. "Here are the tennis shoes we promised to deliver to you today. I got a really good deal on them for you."

"Gentlemen," Mr. Lozinski said, "come into my office. I'll sign the delivery papers there."

As we walked into the office again, he shut the door behind us. "Good work, boys. That was faster than I expected."

Then he grabbed the telephone and dialed a number. My knees began to shake. Had he set us up?

When someone answered, he said, "Cy, this is Joe Lozinski. Remember those two cases of tennis shoes I ordered the other day? Could you please cancel that order? They're just not moving as quickly as I expected. Maybe in a month or so I'll call and reorder them. Okay?"

With that, he hung up and then opened the bottom drawer of his desk, pulling out a metal box that contained a lot of money. The wheels started turning in my brain. We ought to come back here some night and get that little metal box!

Mr. Lozinski counted out two hundred dollars and handed it to Oscar, who stuffed it into his pocket. I almost started complaining about my cut, but I decided to shut up for now. It might make the guy nervous. He might even pull a gun and take it back. Or he might call the cops and say we were trying to sell him stolen goods!

We shook hands all around. Mr. Lozinski was grinning like a kid who had just been told he didn't have to go to school today. I knew he must have been thinking about the good money he was going to make on the deal.

When we got back out on the street, I said to Oscar, "I know we just stole two cases of tennis shoes, and I think I know why."

"I knew you were smart enough to figure it out, Lefty," Oscar said. "You know, I think everybody in this world is crooked. Some of these businessmen I know are crooked, and I pull some deals for them. These businessmen order some tennis shoes or whatever. They know when to expect the delivery truck. Then they work with guys like you and me to steal the merchandise before it's delivered. Now Lozinski would probably have to pay four hundred dollars or so for those tennis shoes wholesale—those are really expensive shoes. Instead, he pays us one hundred dollars a case and saves himself three hundred right off the top. He sells them at the regular price and makes even more."

"You mean there are other guys who operate this way, too?" I asked in unbelief.

"Yes, there sure are. Guys like Lozinski say that the delivery companies have insurance against theft, so the wholesaler isn't out anything. Insurance pays it all. You know, everybody's got an excuse for what they do. But I say they're all a bunch of crooks, whatever they call it."

I wasn't about to argue that point, but I also decided something else. I had to get into this kind of business. It seemed so simple—and so quick. Just think—each of us had a hundred bucks for just carrying a couple of cases of tennis shoes a few blocks. At least, I was hoping I had a hundred bucks.

"Hey, Oscar, what about my cut?"

Oscar pulled out five twenties and handed them to me. Wow! This *was* easy!

We took the subway and headed back to our neighborhood. When we got there, Oscar went looking for Spino. I knew what he wanted—the same thing I did. We both needed to get off.

It didn't take long to locate Spino this time. He acted as though nothing had happened yesterday. We copped and then headed back to Oscar's "paradise"—that filthy, dirty tenement.

Oscar had an extra set of works that I had to buy from him for ten dollars. But at that point I wasn't about to argue.

After we got off, we went back out into the street. As we stood there nodding, a mailman headed our way.

Oscar nudged me. "Hey, see that mailman? I know him. I mean, this guy has a deal going that you won't believe. I think he's going to make us a lot of money. And I do mean a *lot* of money!"

A mailman, able to make us a lot of money? That didn't make sense to me. But Oscar was right about this one. He made us a bundle. It was quite a scheme!

5

As the mailman came nearer, I became suspicious. No mailbag? That didn't fit.

He was about five feet away when Oscar called, "Hey, Jerome. What's up, man?"

"Hey, Oscar, old buddy. I've been living on top of the world, man," Jerome responded.

By this time they were slapping each other on the back like a couple of college chums. But I knew Oscar sure hadn't been to any college. Like me, he had dropped out of high school.

Then Oscar remembered me and he said, "Jerome, this is my buddy Lefty. He's rooming with me. Lefty, this is Jerome Atkins."

We shook hands, but Jerome never would look me straight in the eye. Strange.

"Say, Jerome, are you making lots of money for the post office?" Oscar asked with a laugh.

"Yeah, man," Jerome responded. "They like me so well that one of these days I'll be the postmaster general in Washington, D.C. I'll be a really big dude in that town. I'll get a chauffeured limousine, and I'll deliver the mail personally to the president! What do you think of that?"

The two of them laughed at that as though their sides would split. So far I was totally on the outside of this conversation, and I didn't see anything funny about it at all. But I was kind of embarrassed to be on the outside, so I laughed anyway.

"Hey, Jerome," Oscar said, lowering his voice to a confidential tone, "how would you like to make a little extra money?"

Jerome shifted his gaze to the dirty sidewalk. Then he looked up the street. What was going on?

When he didn't respond, Oscar repeated, "Hey, man, what's with you? I asked if you wanted to make some money. I mean, big money. Really big money—and easy."

Jerome still kept looking down the street. Then he started shifting from one foot to another, obviously very nervous about something or other.

Finally, without ever looking at Oscar, he replied, "How?"

"Man, I think you know," Oscar replied. "Now I know you sort in the mail room. So listen closely, and this can make you a bundle. While you're sorting through all that mail, every time you feel a piece of hard plastic inside an envelope, just slip it in your pocket. And if the envelope looks as though it contains a check, slip that in, too. Then you bring them to me. I'll give you twenty percent on all the checks and twenty-five dollars each for those plastic credit cards. Before you know it, you'll be rolling in dough! Now isn't that easy?"

"You have to be kidding!" Jerome responded indignantly. "Oscar, that's against the law!"

"Against the law?" Oscar sneered. "What do you mean, against the law? Here I am out in the street starving to death. Lefty and I don't even have enough money to buy a Coney Island hot dog. You should see the dump I have to live in. I mean, it's the basement of that tenement house right over there." He pointed. "It reeks of garbage. It's overrun with rats and roaches. And you can stand there and tell me that this little caper is against the law? How come the law isn't doing anything to help me? How come it isn't arresting these businessmen who are always ripping off little guys like me? How come? How come?"

By this time Oscar's finger was jabbing into Jerome's chest to punctuate his arguments. He sure sounded convincing. But I knew Oscar wasn't looking for money to buy food. Every penny he got would go to buy drugs.

Jerome obviously was having quite a struggle.

"I have to think of my job, Oscar," he said. "And of my family. My wife's pregnant, and if I—"

"That's what I want you to do—think of your family," Oscar interrupted. "Think of all the extra things you'll be able to buy for them with the money you'll make on this deal. Think of all the toys you can buy for that baby. Maybe you can even take your wife out to a swanky restaurant for dinner. How about it, man?"

That must have convinced him, for he said, somewhat reluctantly, "Okay, man. I sure can't do anything for my kids on my salary. I'll try it. I'll meet you here tomorrow at this same time. But be sure you have your money with you. And so help me, if either of you breathes a word about this to anybody, you're both dead! I mean, real dead!"

He turned on his heels and walked off, without another word.

Oscar was all smiles, anticipating the money he was going to get from selling the stuff Jerome brought him. But I wasn't so sure it was that good an idea.

"I smell a rat, Oscar," I said. "I don't think that Jerome guy will go through with it. I'll bet that tomorrow at work he'll tell his supervisor, and the supervisor will tell the FBI, and they'll set us up. Then it'll be the slammer!"

"Oh, for crying our loud, Lefty, you are entirely too nervous," Oscar replied. "Sure, it's a bit of a chance, but you have to take chances to make money. We took a chance when we heisted those cases of tennis shoes."

He paused and let that sink in. "Besides, it's not much of a chance with Jerome. We went to school together, and he always was a decent guy. Let me tell you something else, Lefty. Everybody needs a little extra money. Nobody ever has quite enough. Jerome's got three kids and another one on the way. On his salary it takes it all to feed and clothe them. Notice how he fell for my plan when I mentioned what he would be able to do for his kids?"

"Okay, so Jerome probably won't turn us in. But what are you going to do with credit cards and checks? Spino won't take them for dope."

Oscar laughed at that idea. "No, Spino won't take them. But I know somebody who will. Those credit cards are valuable, and I can get maybe forty or fifty percent on those checks!"

"Where?"

"You know Antonio? The one who has that grocery store?"

"Sure, I know him. He's been there for years. So?"

"Antonio is a fence," Oscar whispered.

"What?" I asked in astonishment. "No way! The Antonio I know is as straight as can be. He's no fence."

Oscar named the address. Yes, that was the same Antonio. I couldn't believe he was dishonest.

"He used to be straight," Oscar said. "But business is bad in the ghetto. He got ripped off a number of times and couldn't buy any insurance. He couldn't make ends meet. So he had to join the neighborhood. Now he's the official fence."

I had lived in this neighborhood all my life and didn't know that. Suddenly I felt a little more secure being with Oscar. He seemed to have all the answers, and he always seemed ready to include me in his plans.

"Hey, let's go find Spino and celebrate our good fortune," Oscar said. I was all for that.

Spino was around in the usual area. He seemed surprised to see us again so soon.

"We need four bags, man," Oscar announced. "Two each."

Spino reached inside his coat. "Delivered. Sixty bucks."

We each peeled off thirty dollars and stuffed the packets in our pockets.

"Lefty," Spino said, "you did learn your lesson, didn't you? Remember, don't ever come to my apartment."

"Man, how could I?" I responded. "I don't have an idea in the world where you live. How could I possibly come there?"

"Good boy," Spino responded.

We turned to leave, but Spino called us back. "Listen, I want to tell you two guys something," he said.

I spun around. Was he going to have his brutes jump us again? Was he never going to forget the mistake we had made in going to his apartment? That was Oscar's fault. He shouldn't have taken me there. I didn't ask to go.

Spino was just barely talking above a whisper. "I don't know where or how you're getting your money," he said, "but I'm going to warn you. There are narcos all over the place—a lot of them as decoys. These detectives won't stop at anything!"

"Don't worry, Spino," Oscar said with a laugh. "You mean those cops dressed up as old men and young kids and hot-dog vendors? We know all about them, don't we, Lefty?"

Oscar knew all about them, but I was learning. So I nodded.

"That isn't all, mister," Spino continued. "The detectives are getting so strong in this neighborhood that they are talking to people and setting up lookouts. You know, this neighborhood is getting fed up with crime. People are rising up and offering to be police lookouts to get the junkies. The heat is really on, so you guys be doubly sure before you try anything. Get me?"

Now I was really worried. Jerome might be in with the cops. So I said, "Spino, how about mailmen? Do you think they would pose as lookouts for the cops?"

"No," Spino replied. "What they are looking for are ministers, social workers, people like that. You know—the do-gooders."

That reassured me. Maybe Jerome was okay, after all.

As we walked away, I said, "Oscar, I'm sure glad Spino said what he did."

"What do you mean?" Oscar asked in surprise. "You mean you're glad our neighborhood is swarming with narcos? Don't you know what that's going to do to us? Lefty, we're really up against it. If the heat gets too bad, Spino will disappear. So will every other dealer on the streets. And where will that leave us?"

"No, no," I responded, "that's not what I'm glad about. I'm glad Spino said what he did about mailmen. I was really worried about Jerome."

We walked in silence for a while. I could tell Oscar was thinking about something.

Finally he said, "Lefty, when Spino mentioned that the narcos were swarming in the neighborhood, I thought of Jerome, too. Maybe they did get to him. Maybe they sent him out as a decoy to get junkies like us. Maybe he's really joined the FBI and is only posing as a mailman. Maybe he can get some kind of a reward for turning us in and saying we tried to get him to steal from the U.S. mails. Maybe—"

"That's it! That's it!" I interrupted. "I'm not going to get involved in anything that has to do with Jerome. I didn't like his shifty looks to start with. You know, Oscar, that character never would look me straight in the eye. I'm telling you, he was setting us up. No way am I going to be there tomorrow when he shows up. No way!"

Oscar grabbed me and started to shake me. "Lefty! Lefty! Don't act that way! I was just laying it on thick. I really don't believe all that stuff I said. I know Jerome is a mailman. I've seen him working at the post office. Besides, you heard what Spino said. Jerome's okay."

He let go of me because I was squirming so. Then he lowered his voice and said, "Lefty, we can make thousands on this deal. I mean, there are credit cards going through those mails every day. Everybody has got credit cards. And the checks are there, too. I mean, they are really there. And with the money we get, Lefty, we can go out and buy a mountain of heroin. We can get high and never come down!"

A mountain of heroin. Wow! That was my idea of the highest heaven. For that I'd be willing to take a chance!

"Oscar, where did you ever come up with an idea like this?" I asked.

"Listen, Lefty, I've got two thousand different ideas for making money. This happens to be only one of them. Stick with me, and I'll teach you. Man, we used to have lots of time to rap when I was in prison. And all we talked about was how to make money. Those dudes knew so many ways, it would make your head spin. They said that credit cards and checks are one of the easiest ways—if you have a good fence."

The thought crossed my mind that if all those ways were so easy, what were all those guys doing in prison?

"Are you sure Antonio will take credit cards and checks?"

"Yes," Oscar responded. "I've taken other things to him.

And I already asked him about credit cards and checks. He said he'd take them. I'd already cleared that before I talked to Jerome."

I didn't tell Oscar, but that bit of information made me all the more uneasy. Suppose the cops had gotten to Antonio. He could have told them of Oscar's plan. Then they could have gotten Jerome to come by Oscar's apartment. Maybe he would have brought up the subject if Oscar hadn't. Maybe it was a setup!

But by this time we were back at the apartment, and then there was only one thing on my mind. I wanted to get off again. And by now I knew better than to shoot off more than one bag.

We got off and just sat around the apartment nodding.

Suddenly I was aware of someone knocking on the apartment door. I looked over at Oscar. He was too out of it to be aware of anything.

Who in the world would be out there? Maybe a couple of junkies had seen us cop from Spino and were coming to rip us off. Should I answer the door or ignore the sound?

Someone knocked again—louder, more persistent.

I thought of the other bag still in my pocket. I wasn't about to answer the door with dope in my pocket. So I pulled the bag out, reached for an empty can, and put it in the can. Then I stuffed some papers on top of it and put it with the rest of the garbage.

I staggered to the door. When I finally opened it, I saw a nice-looking couple waiting there.

The girl smiled. "Sir, we're sorry to disturb you, but my husband and I are desperate to find a place to rent. Is this apartment available? Somebody said they thought it was."

My dope-befuddled mind noticed the guy was dressed in a sweatshirt and dungarees—clean ones! She had on a nice-looking skirt and blouse. And then the wheels started to turn. They looked so young, so innocent—so stupid! Maybe Oscar and I could rip them off!

"Hey, man, just a minute," I said. "I have to ask the guy who rents this apartment."

I shut the door and went back over to where Oscar was still nodding. I shook him, and he slowly looked up, his eyes glassy.

"Oscar," I said, "there's a guy and gal outside that door. They want to rent this apartment! Why don't we ask them for a deposit? Then we can see how much money they have, and we can mug them."

"What? What did you say?"

"I said there's a couple out there wanting to rent this apartment. Let's grab them."

"Yeah, man," Oscar responded, coming back to reality a little. "We'll need to cop tomorrow. Let's do it."

I looked around for something to hit them with and spotted Oscar's crowbar in the litter. I'd better take it. I couldn't count on Oscar's hitting anything. He was still too high.

As we headed for the door, I whispered, "You open the door. When they walk in, I'll hit the guy on the back of the head. You take the woman."

Oscar put his hand on the doorknob and looked to see whether I was ready. I gripped the end of the crowbar tightly. I was going to have to hit quickly and hard.

Oscar slowly opened the door about halfway. Suddenly he slammed it, grabbed the crowbar out of my hand, and jammed it against the door. Then he locked the door.

"Those two are cops!" he screamed.

"What?" I yelled. "They can't be cops! They look too clean, too innocent!"

The two must have heard us yelling, for somebody started pounding on the door and yelling, "Okay, you two junkies, open this door. This is the police!"

"What are we going to do now?" I wailed.

"Nothing," Oscar replied. "They probably have backups. It's all over."

"But what do you think they want us for?"

"I don't know," Oscar replied, "but the only thing we can do is open that door."

I quickly threw the crowbar down the hall. Then Oscar undid the latches and slowly opened the door.

Both of them stood there, their guns drawn. Someday, I thought, I would wise up. These two innocent-looking people were narcos!

They pushed their way in. I couldn't help but think how different that girl looked now—especially with that revolver in her hand!

"Okay, you two, march in there," the officer said. By this time Oscar and I had our hands in the air and obediently followed his orders.

"Face the wall and spread-eagle against it," the woman yelled. We both put our hands on the wall and spread our feet apart. The guy grabbed my hands, spun me around, and then I heard that click. Handcuffed. He put cuffs on Oscar, too.

He shoved us back against the wall and demanded, "Okay, where is he?"

I looked at Oscar, and he looked at me. We both drew blanks.

"What do you mean, where is he?" I asked. "Who are you looking for?"

"Okay, boys," the woman cop said, "let's not play games. You cooperate with us, and everything will be all right. If you don't cooperate, you're going to be in big trouble. So tell us, where is he?"

That made Oscar mad. "Listen, cops, I don't know what

you're doing here or what you're looking for. But don't you know you're supposed to have a search warrant before you come into somebody's apartment? Don't you understand that?"

The woman reached into her purse, flipped out some papers, and held them in front of Oscar's face. Search warrants!

But who were they looking for? They had both of us. Who else did they want?

"Who are you looking for?" I asked again.

"Cut out the innocent act," the guy yelled. "You two know very well who we're looking for."

Well, I sure didn't know. Was there somebody else who lived with Oscar? I hadn't been here long. But when I looked at Oscar questioningly, he just shrugged his shoulders.

"We're looking for Spino," the woman cop said. "You know who Spino is?"

Now what was I going to say? If I admitted I knew Spino and they nailed him because of me, then it would be all over for me. Someday Spino would get out, and the first guy he would look for would be me. Or he'd send his bodyguards out looking for me. I had no choice in this one. I had to play dumb.

"We're asking you two guys a question," the man yelled. "Where's Spino?"

I shrugged. So did Oscar.

"All right, you two junkies," the man went on. "We know you know him. We saw you talking to him a little while ago. I understand you two are friends of his. Well, we are looking for him, and we're going to get him. This is our first stop. So why don't you just cooperate and tell us where he is and save yourselves a lot of hassle."

"Hey, man, you've got us all wrong," I said. "We're not

harboring any criminal in this filthy place. It's bad enough having the rats around. You think I like to live like this? My old lady threw me out, and my friend here took me in. I have nowhere else I can go. So I tell you, and I tell you the truth, there isn't anybody else here but us two—plus a few thousand roaches."

The woman cop kept us covered while her partner started checking the rooms. When he came back, he seemed a little more subdued. "I'll have to agree with you," he said. "This place is filthy. It stinks. I don't think Spino would stay around a mess like this. He's got more class."

With that he unlocked both sets of handcuffs, stuffed them into his pocket, and said to his partner, "Come on. Let's get out of here. Maybe we'll catch him on the street."

As soon as they were out the door, I slammed it and locked it.

"Wow!" Oscar said, "That was close! Can you imagine what would have happened if we had tried to mug them? You and your bright ideas."

"Okay, okay," I responded. "So I goofed again. But for crying out loud, where did you get the ability to know cops that way?"

Oscar shrugged. "Experience, I guess. It's something that's there. It just seems I can smell them!"

"If you're so good," I said, "what about Jerome?"

"Lefty, I wish you would quit bringing up Jerome. He's a nice guy. I know him personally, and in no way would he ever rat on us."

"Don't be too sure, Oscar. This neighborhood is swarming with informers. Even Spino knows that. And they know who Spino is!"

"Lefty, Lefty, quit your worrying. It'll make an old man out of you. Everything will be okay. Besides, this is a good way to make money. It's a lot safer than muggings—especially with cops swarming all over the neighborhood. Muggings never bring us much, anyway. But Jerome will be a good connection that'll bring us money every single day. You watch. Tomorrow Jerome will bring us a stack of credit cards and checks. I'll take them to Antonio, get our money, and we can live happily ever after."

"Yes, but we're supposed to have the money to give to Jerome when he comes tomorrow. Do you have extra money? I don't."

"No, but I know Jerome. I'll just put him off. I'll tell him I'll pay him as soon as I get some money from Antonio. Guys like Jerome are easy to work a deal with. Besides, what's he going to do with them? He certainly can't take them back to the post office. And he'll be nervous about having them on him. He'll be an easy setup. No problem."

Oscar made it all sound so easy, so simple. But why did I have this nagging feeling that something was wrong, really wrong?

We went out on the streets and hung around for a while, then went back to our filthy apartment and slept. We got off again the next morning and sat around nodding and scratching, waiting for the time Jerome had said he'd show up.

Maybe it was just the anticipation of the deal, but I was still nervous. Finally four o'clock came—the time Jerome was supposed to arrive. Oscar went out on the street and then came back in and reported he couldn't see Jerome anywhere. We both went outside and waited. No Jerome.

The waiting was killing me. So I said, "Oscar, I don't know if it's me or if we're being set up. But I'm still uneasy about this whole deal." I glanced around, somehow expecting cops to be headed our way.

"What do you want me to do about it?" Oscar asked. "Call the whole thing off? Man, we're going to make good money out of this one. This will be a pipeline to thousands of dollars, and we'll live like kings. Now if you're chicken and want out, just walk down that street and forget the whole thing. But I'm staying here and waiting."

"Oscar, don't get me wrong," I said. "I think it's a fantastic idea. But I'm just nervous about it. I sure hope we don't get busted. This is a federal offense."

"Okay, if it'll make you a little calmer, this is what we can do," Oscar said. "I'll go up on the rooftop and watch Jerome come. If I spot any narcos or other cops around, I'll yell, 'Raisin bread'—just like before."

"Hey, wait a minute!" I protested. "You know what's going to happen then? You'll yell and run. But I'll be standing right there, and those narcos will grab me and send me away. No way, man. Jerome is your friend. He'll deal with you. Let me be the lookout."

"For crying out loud, Lefty, I can't take that kind of a chance," Oscar replied. "From what I've seen of your ability so far, you couldn't tell a narco from a telephone pole. No, it has to be me on the lookout. I promise if I spot somebody suspicious, I'll yell. If Jerome starts to hand you something, look up at me. If I give you the salute, it's okay to go ahead with the deal. If I don't, then don't touch anything. They won't bust you if you don't put your hands on it. If it's a trap, it's probably marked—maybe they might have powder on it. So before you touch anything, look four floors up. As I say, if it's okay, I'll salute. If it's not, I'll be screaming my head off. And you run for it. But remember, don't touch it. Those cops are smart enough to know not to bust you until you have it in your hands. They have to catch you with it on you."

That sounded like good sense. I knew I couldn't spot a narco in disguise the way Oscar could, so I had to trust him.

"Okay, I guess you're right, Oscar," I said. "But so help

me, if you ever put your instinct to good use, do it now! If you blow this one, I'll see you in prison."

"Don't talk that way, Lefty," Oscar warned. "Don't ever mention prison. It can bring you bad luck."

Oscar ran inside the tenement. I could hear him pounding up the stairs. I looked down the street. Still no sign of Jerome. Then I looked up. Still no sign of Oscar, either. Had he taken off?

Then I noticed two little old ladies heading my way. Could it be they were cops in disguise?

I looked straight up again. Whew! There was Oscar leaning over the side. He saluted. Everything was clear so far.

He pointed down the street. That's when I spotted Jerome heading toward me. As he got closer, I could see he was grinning. But the closer he got, the more nervous I got. I just knew something terrible was about to happen!

6

The way Jerome was grinning, he must have the credit cards and checks on him. I could see that mountain of heroin beginning to materialize. Maybe my fears were groundless, after all.

I glanced up at Oscar to get the salute I almost knew was coming. I couldn't see him! Oscar! Oscar! Where was he? Why would he disappear at this critical moment? He wouldn't play games with me, would he?

The closer Jerome got, the more frantic I became in trying to locate Oscar. He certainly wasn't peering over the roof edge as he had been a moment ago. Now what was I going to do?

Jerome was beside me now. He didn't even ask where Oscar was. As he reached into his pocket, he said, "Hey, man, this was a lot easier than I thought. Would you believe I got ten credit cards today? Hey, man, look!"

He stood there holding out the plastics, but I couldn't look. My eyes were searching upward frantically, hoping for some sign from Oscar—or some sign *of* Oscar! Why had he run out on me now? Did he suspect something and take off, leaving me to face the music alone?

I started to turn, but Jerome grabbed my shoulder with his free hand. "Hey, man, why so nervous? I got you what you asked for. Ten big ones. And, man, I got checks, too—a whole stack of them. Partner, we're in business. Big business!"

If Jerome had become an undercover agent, he sure was faking it well. He sounded so excited about what he had done. But what should I do? Should I go ahead and take the stuff? Maybe Oscar was just lighting a cigarette or something. I'd better stall.

Jerome fanned the ten cards out. I'd never had a credit card, so I didn't know one from another, but I said, "Wow! You sure got some good ones there. Are you sure they're brand-new?"

"Yes," Jerome responded, "absolutely brand-new. These babies never saw the light of day before I pulled them out of their envelopes just a little while ago. I'll bet these will make somebody a pile of money, right?"

"Yes. Right, Jerome." My thoughts drifted to Antonio's grocery store, where we could cash these in, get our money, and buy our dope. If I did that by myself, that sure would make Oscar happy. But where was he? Why wasn't he giving me some signal—one way or the other?

"Okay, man, how much money will you give me for these cards and these checks? Oscar said something like twenty percent on the checks and twenty-five dollars each for the cards. That'll be. . . ."

At this point I had no idea how much it would be. I still had to stall, because Oscar had completely disappeared.

"Hey, what's the matter, man?" Jerome asked. "You sure are jumpy. You think the cops will get us or something?"

I studied the street closely. Nobody around seemed out of the ordinary. Just neighborhood people who were part of the street scene. If the cops wanted to bust me, I couldn't see where they would come from. But then I had been wrong about the cops too many times before!

Yet, maybe Jerome was clean. After all, he was Oscar's buddy. He wouldn't turn Oscar in, would he? And he probably did need the extra money Oscar promised him.

But should I take the chance? Oscar had warned me that whatever I did, I shouldn't touch these cards, because as soon as I did, they would become my property. And that's when they could bust me.

Still stalling, I asked Jerome, "Have you seen Oscar around?"

"No, man. He's your friend. I expected him to be here with you."

"We have a little problem here, Jerome. He was supposed to meet me here. I haven't seen him for a while, so I thought maybe you saw him along the way somewhere."

Jerome kept assuring me he hadn't seen Oscar.

"Well, Jerome," I said, "you know how it is. I just don't dare take these credit cards and checks from you. After all, this was Oscar's idea. He might think I was trying to double-cross him. And you know Oscar. Nobody double-crosses him and gets by with it." I let that statement sink in. "I mean, if we did, he'd follow us both and blow our brains out."

"Hey, no problem, no problem," Jerome responded. "I know Oscar, and he knows me. I'll explain everything to him the next time I see him. All you have to do is give me some money for these, and we're on our way. Oscar will understand that you're not double-crossing him. No problem at all."

"Okay, Jerome, but there's something else. You told Oscar to be sure to bring the money with him. I don't have any on me. Oscar's got the money." I knew that was a lie, but if Oscar showed up, we could come up with another one.

"All I can do," I continued, "is to take these credit cards and checks to a fence. Then when I get the money, I'll come back and split it with you."

I knew that would turn Jerome off. Nobody on the streets trusts anybody else—especially a junkie. I knew Jerome would turn me down on that. But I couldn't help but think that if he trusted me, what a fabulous system it would be! I would make money and Jerome would make money. So would Oscar. That mountain of heroin started to become a reality again. What a time we'd have shooting it all up. But I knew it was only a dream. Jerome wasn't about to surrender those cards and checks unless he saw hard cash.

I guess that's why I was so shocked when he said, "No problem, man; no problem whatsoever. As I say, I know Oscar; now I know you. Any friend of Oscar's has got to be a friend of mine. So you just take these, and I'll sit here on the steps and wait until you get back. Okay?"

I glanced up again. Still no Oscar.

"Jerome, I just can't do it without Oscar. But I'll make

you a deal. I'll tell you where you can take them to the fence. You get seventy-five percent of the take and give me twenty-five percent for the information. How's that for a deal?"

"What?" Jerome yelled. "What are you talking about, man? Are you standing there telling me that if I take these to a fence and cash them, I'm supposed to come back here and give you twenty-five dollars for each hundred bucks I get? You crazy or something?"

"Okay, okay," I responded. "You don't have to get mad about it. If you don't want to do it, you don't have to. Okay?"

"You'd better believe I won't do it!" he retorted. "I wish you could have seen my hands trembling when I took the first card off that conveyor belt. I kept touching all those letters, and I finally felt one, and there was that hard part. I glanced around, and no one was looking, so I slipped the thing in my pocket. I was shaking so badly and sweating so much that you'd have thought I just got out of the shower!"

He sure was making me believe he really had stolen them!

"The second one wasn't quite as difficult as the first one," he went on. "Then it got easier and easier. But, man, when I walked out of that post office this afternoon, I knew everybody was staring holes through me. At any minute I expected someone to stop me and tell me they knew what I was doing. Man, I've been honest all my life. I've never done anything like this before. I got to thinking about why I was doing it—to make a little extra money for my kids— and then I wondered whether it was worth it. What good will it do them if their old man ends up in jail?"

By this time Jerome was really getting agitated about the whole situation. "In fact, man," he shouted, "if you don't take these right this minute, I'll turn around and take off.

I'll cut these cards to shreds and toss them into the garbage. So if you're chickening out of this deal, I won't do something like this for you ever again. I've had it. I mean, I've really had it. So you either take these now, or you can forget this forever!"

I couldn't bear to see that mountain of heroin disappear. Jerome had to be on the level. I had no doubt about it now.

"Okay, cool it, Jerome. I didn't mean to get you so upset. But let me level with you."

"Level with me? What you talking about, man?"

"Oscar and I were talking about something. You see, lately it seems that every time we turn around, we're running into these undercover cops. They're everywhere. And last night Oscar and I talked about you, Jerome. Now don't get mad again, but let me tell you something. We have to be extra cautious because we can't afford to get busted. Well, when Oscar and I were talking, the subject came up, Is Jerome on the level? The more we talked, the more we wondered. Now as I say, man, don't get mad, but we worried that maybe you'd get cold feet and tell the cops about the deal. Maybe you could even be an undercover cop yourself. Know what I mean?"

The more I talked, the madder Jerome got. "You dirty, good-for-nothing junkie," he yelled. "How do I know *you* didn't go to the cops? How do I know they didn't hire a couple of junkies to help them make arrests in the post office? No employee would ever suspect junkies of working for the cops, would they? Why, you dirty double-crosser! I know all about undercover cops. Do you know what those cops do sometimes?"

I shrugged. I had no idea what he was driving at.

"Well, I'll tell you, Lefty. Those cops bust a guy. Then they tell him he can go free if he rats on his friends. And I think you'd do that to me, man.

"I'll tell you something else, Lefty. Stealing from the post office isn't something new. We get warned about it all the time. I know all that. But as I told you guys yesterday, I need some extra cash. With three kids and a pregnant wife, there's no way I can pay all my bills on what I'm making. Here I was willing to take a big chance to get some money. I didn't want to do it. I was scared. Now I find out that you're probably an FBI agent planted to get me to do something wrong. Lefty, I think you stink!"

With that, he flung the cards down at his feet in disgust.

Well, I blew up, too. "Jerome," I shouted, "I don't mind your calling me a few bad words, but I don't want you to read me wrong! So we suspected you. And you have every right to suspect us. Nobody can trust anybody. But there's no point in getting mad about it. You can't blame me for being cautious. Suppose I did get busted. Do you know what that means? I'd be slapped away in the slammer for years!"

As we argued back and forth, a man walked by, stopped, and looked down at the credit cards. I started to stoop and pick them up, but something inside me said, *Stop! Don't do it while he's watching!*

Jerome didn't make any effort to pick them up. He just stood there with his arms folded over his chest and his feet spread apart—really defiant.

I straightened up, but nobody said anything. Who was this guy, anyway? Something about him wasn't right.

Finally I said, "Can I help you, sir?"

No answer. He just stood there, staring, first down at the cards, then at me. If Jerome and this guy were up to no good, I wasn't about to touch those cards!

"Hey, man, you'd better pick up your credit cards," I said to Jerome. "Your wife might want to use them again."

I laughed as though it were kind of a funny joke. But neither Jerome nor the guy cracked a smile.

Something was wrong. My heart responded to the uncertainty by beating a mile a minute. I knew the old adrenaline was flowing—just in case I needed to run.

"Mister, do you want a credit card?" I asked.

He looked me over carefully. Then he studied the cards. I sensed he was going to go after them.

Just as he bent over, I pushed him as hard as I could. He went sprawling across the sidewalk and banged his head against a parked car. I took off running as fast as I could.

Halfway down the block I ducked inside a tenement and hit the stairs to run to the roof as fast as I could. When I got there, I edged close to the side and looked down at where I had been a few moments before. There I saw Jerome and the guy I had bumped picking up the credit cards. And surrounding them were five cops! It was a setup!

As I stared down in disbelief, Jerome handed the cards to one of the officers. Another one shook Jerome's hand. That dirty rat! My suspicions were right! He had become an FBI informer! And I almost got busted!

Busted! The word itself almost made me sick. I thought of what prison would be like. No drugs, no freedom!

Just then I spotted two cops come out of the building where we had been standing. Someone was between them, squirming and cursing. I couldn't believe it. They had Oscar! No wonder I hadn't been able to see him!

Even from that distance I could hear him yelling, "Let me go! Let me go! I don't know what you're talking about. You don't have anything on me!"

Although Oscar was handcuffed, he kept jumping up and down. They brought him over by Jerome. I couldn't hear what was said, but Jerome pointed at Oscar, and

Oscar let loose and tried to kick him. The officers quickly threw Oscar up against the building. I could see an officer shaking his finger at Oscar, and I could hear Oscar still shouting and cursing.

So they had Oscar. My knees buckled as I realized how close I had come to getting busted, too!

I heard a siren and looked around to see a police car drive up, red lights flashing. Four officers got out. There was a lot more animated conversation which I couldn't hear. But I was thinking about poor Oscar. He'd probably get fifteen years for this. But they didn't really have anything on him, did they? It would be his word against Jerome's.

They kept yelling back and forth, but finally one of the officers went over and took off the handcuffs. Another one kept pointing his finger at Oscar and yelling. I moved closer and closer, trying to catch their words. The officer seemed to be telling Oscar that they might have failed to catch him this time, but they were going to get him.

Oscar kept yelling at the top of his lungs, so I could hear him. "I don't know what you're talking about," he shouted. "All I was doing was getting some fresh air up there on the rooftop. Then these two jerks grabbed me and gagged me. That's all I know, man!"

Then I heard another officer yell, "Get out of here, kid. I don't ever want to see your face around here again!"

He didn't have to say that a second time because Oscar took off like a scared cat. I watched as the officers dispersed. Finally Jerome started down the street by himself.

I ran across a couple of tenement roofs. Oscar was probably headed back to the apartment. I exited on the other side of the block and hurried back to my new home.

Oscar was already there. Oh, he was mad. "I'll kill him!"

he screamed. "I'll kill him! That dirty, filthy rat! Lefty, he almost sent us away for fifteen years. I'll kill him!"

I had never seen him so enraged. "Cool it, man; cool it!" I said. "We can come to that later. Tell me what went wrong."

"I got up to the rooftop all right," he said. "You saw me salute you. Well, those two cops came up from behind and threw me down on the roof. Before I knew what was happening, they had those cuffs on me. I tried to scream, and they gagged me. I was scared to death about what was happening to you, man, but there was nothing I could do. I was sure hoping you would play it cool, man."

"So help me, Oscar, I almost took those credit cards. It's a good thing you had warned me about not touching them. That saved my skin. I mean, Jerome sounded so convincing. I almost fell for his trap."

"And I thought I could trust Jerome," Oscar told me. "I guess he must have gotten cold feet. Or maybe they caught him and made a deal with him to try to get us."

Oscar was pacing like a tiger in a cage. "When I get through with that rat, he'll wish he had never tried to double-cross us!" Oscar threatened.

"Are you really going to kill him?"

"I don't know. The way I feel now, I'm going to cut him up and make him suffer. Then if I feel like stabbing him to death, I just might do it. I can't stand a rat."

"Oscar, you wouldn't kill a guy, would you?"

"No, I wouldn't kill a guy, but I might kill a rat," Oscar snarled.

I was about as angry as Oscar was. Maybe we really did need to teach Jerome a lesson. And that would be a warning to neighborhood people who tried to turn us junkies in to the police.

In a few minutes Oscar was beginning to calm down and think a little more rationally. "I'll tell you what, Lefty," he said. "We'll stay cool until late tonight. I know where that rat lives. And we are going to pay him a little visit. We'll have a little classroom there in his apartment, and we'll be the teachers. He has to be taught. You know, Lefty, as soon as guys like that are afraid of you, they'll do anything. We might get something out of this deal yet."

"Yeah, man," I responded. "I'm with you. Let's teach that rat a lesson."

We waited until about 2:00 A.M., then made our way to Jerome's apartment on 114th Street. Oscar said he lived on the fourth floor of the tenement—apartment 401.

When we got there, Oscar knocked. No answer. He banged.

Then we heard a sleepy voice ask, "Yes, who is it?"

Oscar disguised his voice. "Mr. Jerome Atkins? This is Officer Reed from the local precinct. I have Officer Gosler with me. Can we talk with you a minute?"

From behind the door Jerome responded, "What seems to be the problem? Isn't it something that can wait until morning?"

"Some of our men were out in the street tonight. We understand from our connections that two guys named Oscar and Lefty are headed this way. We thought we'd better come over here and protect you and your family. We don't want anything to happen to you. So I think it's best if you let us spend the night here. Then we'll be ready if those two guys try anything."

I heard him fumbling with some locks, and the door opened. Oscar pushed it wide open, and before Jerome knew what had happened, Oscar had hit him hard in the mouth. Stunned and surprised, Jerome went tumbling backward. Oscar pounced on him like a tiger.

I stepped inside and shut the door.

Oscar was beating on Jerome and yelling, "You dirty rat! You dirty rat! We're here to teach you a lesson. We're going to kill you!" He whipped out his switchblade and waved it menacingly near Jerome's throat.

A woman came running down the hallway, screaming. She was obviously pregnant, so I assumed this must be Jerome's wife.

Oscar looked over his shoulder at her and yelled, "Shut up, woman, or I'll kill you, too!"

He grabbed Jerome by the neck and pulled and pushed him down the hallway to the living room, where he flung him onto the sofa. He tossed his switchblade to me, pulled out his .45 pistol, jumped on top of Jerome and yelled, "Okay, Jerome, tell your little wife good-bye. It's all over for you!" He jammed the gun against Jerome's temple.

Oh, no! I didn't think he was going to kill Jerome. I sure didn't want to be an accomplice to a murder. I thought all we were going to do was to scare Jerome, to teach him a lesson.

"Don't, Oscar! Don't!" I yelled.

Jerome's eyes bugged out in terror. "Please! Have mercy! Please! Let me explain. Please!"

The pregnant wife was screaming and blubbering. I couldn't let Oscar kill Jerome. There was no way we'd ever get out of this one. So I yelled, "Cool it, Oscar! Cool it, man! Let's do what we said and get out of here!"

With all the screaming and shouting going on, it was enough to wake the dead. Oscar yelled at me, "Get that woman out of here. She bugs me."

"Go to your bedroom and stay there and shut up!" I ordered the woman.

She threw her hands in the air and screamed again.

I clapped my hand over her mouth. "You'd better do what he says, lady, or it could be bad for you and your kids. Don't make him any angrier than he already is."

She pulled away and ran down the hall, sobbing. At least she wasn't screaming.

"Jerome, I ought to pull this trigger and splatter your brains all over this pillow," Oscar said. "But I'll tell you something. I'm going to spare your life this time."

I felt great relief when I heard that. But I guess Jerome must have been even more relieved. "Hey, man, I really appreciate that," he mumbled.

"Not so fast!" Oscar yelled. "I mean, like man, you almost sent me away for fifteen years. I can't stand a rat. I'm going to make a deal with you, but I'm not going to give you a choice. You'll have to promise to do what I say, or it's all over for you, man."

Oscar still had the gun against Jerome's temple, and the poor man squirmed a little, trying to get away from it. "What do you want me to do, man?" he asked nervously. "Anything. Anything."

"Tomorrow you're going to go back to that post office and you're going to steal some more credit cards and checks," Oscar said. "Only this time you're not going to go to the cops. Understand?"

When Jerome didn't respond, Oscar pushed the gun into his temple again. Jerome's eyes bugged out, and he finally said, "Okay, man, okay. But just cool it. I'll do whatever you say."

"That's better," Oscar responded. "Now this is how we're going to do it. The next time you walk up that street, we won't be standing there to meet you. We're going to—"

Suddenly Mrs. Atkins burst into the room, screaming, "Don't kill! Don't kill! Take these!"

Her outstretched hands were filled with credit cards and checks. Wow! Where had all these come from?

We both turned toward Jerome. "Let me explain," he pleaded. "Just please get that thing away from my head."

Oscar slowly moved the gun back and let Jerome sit up. First there was a deathly silence. The woman broke it with, "Take them! Take them!" She headed toward me and pushed them at me. Instinctively I grabbed, as credit cards and checks tumbled from her arms into mine. Some of them spilled onto the floor. I just couldn't understand. I had seen Jerome give those credit cards to a cop. So where had all these come from?

"Listen, I'll level with you," Jerome said nervously. "This is the truth, the honest truth. You can even ask my wife."

"Hurry it up!" Oscar ordered.

"I've been taking credit cards and checks from the post office for some months now," Jerome said. "It was no problem to steal them. But I didn't know what to do with them. When I saw you, Oscar, and you made that proposition, I already had these cards. My hesitation was that I didn't want to deal with a couple of junkies. I didn't know whether I could trust you. I worried that maybe you'd squeal on me. But I was so desperate for money that I knew I had to do something. So I decided to take a chance."

"Well, why did you bring all those cops along?" Oscar demanded.

"I sure didn't want it that way," Jerome continued. "Let me explain."

I walked over and sat down, my hands still full of those credit cards and checks. I eyed those on the floor. Oscar could get those before we left.

"Yesterday when I was about to leave work," Jerome

went on, "a couple of guys came up to me. They were dressed in suits. Right away I knew who they were—FBI agents. I was shaking like a leaf. I figured they had the goods on me.

"They told me they wanted to talk to me, and they took me to a little office. Talk about scared. I had ten credit cards and about twenty checks on me right then. I was sure they would search me, and that would be it.

"Well, they began to tell me this long story about a lot of stuff being stolen from the post office. They went on and on, and I kept getting more and more nervous. At any moment I expected them to flip out their handcuffs and take me away. Instead, they told me they needed some help in their investigation. They offered me some credit cards to take and go out on the street. If anybody asked me about buying credit cards or checks, all I had to do was give them these, they told me."

"You're lying!" Oscar screamed. "I don't believe one little word you're saying!"

"Oscar, please! I'm telling you the truth!"

"Let's hear him out, Oscar," I said.

"Anyway, I knew I was supposed to meet you guys. Since I was so late, I was hoping you wouldn't be around. But when I saw Lefty, I really didn't know what to do. The cops were tailing me. Maybe they had even put a radio transmitter in those cards. I didn't know. But I knew I had to play it cool or I would be in real trouble—and they'd find out that I was the one who had been stealing the cards."

So that was it. It was beginning to make a little sense.

"I tried hard to get Lefty into an argument," Jerome continued. "Then I deliberately spilled the cards on the street. I was hoping he would see they were fake ones. The FBI supplies them. They're not good for anything.

"All the while I was stalling for time. I knew that if Lefty touched those cards, the cops would appear from everywhere. And then this guy came down the street and stopped. I knew he had to be an FBI agent. So help me, did I ever breathe a sigh of relief when Lefty shoved him and took off."

Oscar turned to me. "Lefty, do you think he's telling the truth?"

"Oscar, I've been fooled before, but this certainly sounds like a good story. I can honestly say that he did try to get me into an argument, and he did throw those cards on the ground. But I don't know anything about credit cards. I don't know whether they were fake. They looked okay to me."

"Okay, Jerome, what did you tell those cops after Lefty took off?" Oscar demanded.

"So help me, this is the truth. I told them, 'Man, I wish you guys had gotten here sooner. I almost had this junkie for you. And when they brought you down, Oscar, I had to accuse you. I had to cover, or they would have suspected me. I knew they really didn't have anything on you and that the case wouldn't hold up in court. You hadn't touched anything. So after that, they shook my hand and thanked me. I came back home. And that's the truth."

"What I don't understand," Oscar said, "is why—"

He was interrupted by someone banging on the apartment door. I sprang to my feet. It must be the cops, and there was no place to go. Now they would catch us red-handed with all these credit cards and checks. Had they staked the place out and set this trap, too? Was there no getting away from them?

Oscar pointed his gun toward the door, then toward Jerome. "If this is a setup," he snarled, "so help me, I'll kill you. If those are cops, there is going to be a shoot-out.

They're not going to take me alive. And you won't be alive when this is over, either!"

Mrs. Atkins gasped, "Please! Please! Don't kill! Don't kill!"

"Shut up, Mrs. Atkins," Oscar ordered. "And walk toward that door. But whatever you do, don't open it. Find out who's there and what they want. If you open it or try anything funny, your sweet husband will be a dead man!"

She inched toward the door, calling, "Who's there, please?"

The suspense was killing me!

Then a woman's voice on the other side called, "Is something the matter?"

I relaxed. Then it hit me. Oh, no! It could be a woman cop!

"No. No. No. No problem," Mrs. Atkins called back. "No problem. No problem."

"I heard all the yelling and screaming," the woman said. "Should I call the cops?"

"No! No! No!" Mrs. Atkins screamed. "No cops. No trouble. No, please don't call! No! No! No!"

She was being too dramatic. With that kind of an answer, the first thing that woman was going to do was call the cops. So I dumped the credit cards and checks on the floor, walked down the hallway, and opened the door.

My gamble paid off, for there stood a lone woman in her robe and slippers. With my biggest smile I said, "Why, hello there! I'm Mrs. Atkins' brother. You see, they were having a little family squabble. You know, the husband-and-wife kind. Well, my sister called me over to help them out. I guess we got kind of noisy shouting back and forth, but I think we are all calmed down now. Sorry we disturbed you. We're a pretty emotional family."

"Oh, just a little family argument?" the woman asked. "I see. I see."

I didn't know whether I had convinced her or not, so I turned and yelled, "Jerome, come on down here and see this kind neighbor who is concerned about you. Tell her everything is okay."

As Jerome came to the door, I put one arm around him and one around Mrs. Atkins. "See, ma'am," I said, "one, big, happy family. Right, Jerome?"

Jerome nodded. At least he was playing along. He probably knew Oscar had that pistol aimed at his back!

The woman looked embarrassed as she said, "Please forgive me. I just thought maybe somebody needed help. You know how it is when you hear a lot of shouting and screaming in the middle of the night. And I thought I heard somebody yell something about killing somebody. I didn't know what was going on, and I just wanted to see if I could help."

"Thank you, ma'am; that really is kind of you," I said. "It's good that there are some people like you who are willing to get involved. But there really isn't any problem here now, and there won't be any more yelling. Right, Jerome?"

I looked over at him and pushed on his back at the same time. "Lefty," he said, "this is our neighbor, Mrs. Fortunato."

"Happy to meet you, Mrs. Fortunato. And I assure you there won't be any more noise."

"Right," Jerome responded, adding, "and we sure thank the good Lord for sending Lefty to help us get this thing settled."

When the woman turned and padded down the hallway toward her apartment, I shut the door and locked it. Whew! That was close! And here was hoping she wouldn't go back to her apartment and call the cops anyway.

Oscar had dashed back into the living room and stood there with all the credit cards and checks in his hands.

"What are you doing?" Jerome asked. "Those are mine!"

"Wrong!" Oscar laughed. "I really ought to kill you, Jerome. I don't know whether I believe your story or not. But I'll tell you this one thing: You're going to pay and pay dearly, for setting up that trap—whether the cops forced you to do it or not. You almost cost me fifteen years out of my life, so I'm going to take all of these as payment for that."

"Please, Oscar, don't do that!" Jerome pleaded. "You have no idea what I had to go through to get those. Ever since I took my first one, it's been hell on earth. Every time there's a knock on the door, I jump. Everywhere I go, I keep turning around, thinking someone is following me. Man, don't take them all. Please don't."

"I'm helping you out," Oscar sneered. "I'm not going to kill you—this time."

Mrs. Atkins had her hand on her mouth and looked as though she was in great pain. Oh, no! What if she went into labor right now?

Oscar had stuffed the credit cards and checks into his pocket. They were really bulging out. Then he started toward the door. I followed. When we got to the door, he called back, "Jerome, you can sleep well tonight. You have no credit cards to worry about. And you can be thankful you're not a dead man!"

As we stepped out into the hallway, I happened to glance to the side and noticed a door slightly ajar. I saw that woman peering out. As soon as her eyes met mine, she slammed the door. I guess she didn't buy my story about the family argument. Had she heard our conversation about the credit cards and checks? Had she already called the cops?

As we headed down the four flights to the street, every step seemed to repeat that question: Will the cops be waiting for us when we get to the street?

7

As we hit the street, there wasn't a soul in sight. You can imagine Oscar and I both let out a sigh of relief. But no sooner had we finished commenting on our good fortune than Oscar said, "Look, Lefty—coming around that corner!"

He didn't have to draw me a picture, for there, driving slowly toward us, was a police car.

"Let's run for it!" I whispered.

"Shut up, Lefty!" Oscar said, pulling on my arm. "As soon as you start running, they'll start chasing. We have to assume they don't have anything on us. So stay cool, man, and nothing will happen."

The police car edged closer and closer, and we kept walking in the direction it was coming from. Pretty soon it was going to be too late to run. But so help me, if that car stopped, I was taking off. I wasn't stupid. First thing they would do would be to frisk Oscar, and he had the goods on him. I'd be held as an accomplice.

The police car was right alongside us now. I tried to ignore it by looking straight ahead, but I kept eyeing it with sideways glances. Every muscle in my body tensed, waiting. . . .

Sure enough, the car stopped, and a cop yelled, "What are you two doing out here in the street this time of night?"

Oscar knew I was ready to take off and grabbed my arm

again. Then he turned to the cop. "Officer, we were just heading home. This is my kid brother, and my old lady's been worried to death about him all night. So to calm her down, I went out looking for him. I just found him and am taking him home."

That Oscar! He was as good at lies as I was. And in this situation I knew I'd better play along.

The officer motioned us over toward the car. Oscar roughly shoved me in front of him as we obeyed. I knew he was trying to hide that bulge in his pocket.

He stayed behind me as he pushed me all the way up to the door of the police car. Then he said, "Here, officer, take him. He's a bad boy. We can't do anything with him."

Oh, no! Don't tell me he was setting me up so that he could go free! Somehow I never had trusted him. He'd do anything to save his own neck.

I tried to jerk away, but Oscar just dug his fingers deeper into my arm.

"Officer," Oscar went on, "my little brother here is the most stubborn guy you could ever imagine. I really think you ought to take him away and lock him in the slammer. I mean, put him away for good and teach him a lesson. Maybe then he'll remember when it's time to come home, and I won't have to go out looking for him in the middle of the night."

I fidgeted some, and I could see the officer smile at what he had figured out was a family spat.

"Young man, what were you doing out so late?" he asked me sternly.

I knew I'd better stay cool, so I replied, "Oh, officer, you know how it is. I was just up visiting my girl friend. I mean, man, we weren't doing anything. If you want me to, I can even take you to her house."

When I realized what I'd said, I got a little worried. Suppose he called my bluff!

Oscar must have figured I was laying it on too thick because he interrupted, "Officer, you know that thing that comes on TV? It says, 'It's ten o'clock. Do you know where your children are?' "

"Yes, I know what you mean. It's surprising how many people pay attention to that thing on TV." Then he chuckled.

Oscar joined his laughter. I really didn't see anything funny, but I figured I'd better laugh, too.

"Well, officer, are you going to take him away?" Oscar said. "Are you going to throw him in the slammer?"

I could detect the sarcasm in Oscar's voice, and I'm sure the officer could, too. The officer figured that what I needed was a scare, so he said, "Well, maybe we should let him go this time. But the next time we catch him, we'll put him away for a hundred years. You get that, young man?"

I nodded, acting as though I were relieved that he wasn't going to put me in jail this time. Then Oscar said, "Thanks, officer. I think that warning is just what he needed." He looked over at me and said, "Now come on, Johnny. And don't try to pull anything on me, or that officer will put you away for a hundred years! Do you understand that?"

"Okay, man, just stay cool," I responded. "Quit treating me like a kid. After all, I'm almost eighteen. If I want to go see my girl friend, I'll go see my girl friend!"

Oscar swung me around, keeping himself close behind me by acting as though he were twisting my arm to make me go home. "Now let's get home!" he yelled.

Behind us I heard the noise of the police car pulling away. But Oscar still kept pushing me until we got to the corner and turned down Madison.

"Wow! That was close!" he exclaimed. "But you dumb nut, you almost blew it with that nonsense about your girl friend. Why did you say all that?"

"For crying out loud, Oscar, I was scared when you pushed me toward the car and told the officer to take me away. I thought maybe you were setting me up!"

"You stupid nut!" Oscar said in disgust. "Did you forget my pockets were bulging with that hot merchandise? I had to keep you up close so he wouldn't notice what I was carrying."

Well, this was one time I had it figured right. And I felt proud of myself because I had played the game.

Down in our apartment, Oscar emptied his pockets of the checks and credit cards. They made quite a little mountain, but I was looking at them and seeing that mountain of heroin!

"Let's stuff this in a bag and take it to our fence," I suggested.

"What's the matter with you, Lefty?" Oscar started in. "Don't you know anything? Antonio isn't open this time of night."

Stupid me. Somehow I thought normal people stayed up as late as we addicts did.

"Antonio will open at seven in the morning," Oscar explained. "And you'll be surprised, Lefty, at the number of people going in and out of his store. You'll see junkies trying to sell merchandise and all sorts of stuff. And you'll see people buying groceries and papers. And Antonio is trying to keep them all happy. It's a wonder that guy doesn't get busted."

Just knowing I was going to be able to get off tomorrow morning made me feel good. I didn't know how much money we'd get for the cards and checks, but I knew it had to be a lot. And I was sure hoping Oscar would split it fifty-fifty.

It wasn't all that long until seven, so we just sat around the apartment and dozed. The next thing I remember, I felt Oscar nudge me. "Okay, Lefty, let's get going," he said. "It's payday, man, payday!"

When we got to Antonio's, I was surprised. People were everywhere. I guess I had expected Oscar to go right up to Antonio and tell him what we had for sale. But Oscar kept stalling—and that made me impatient.

A woman—I guess she was Antonio's wife—kept waiting on customers. Antonio just sort of kept an eye on what was happening.

It seemed as though we had been there for an eternity, so I said impatiently, "Hey, man, what's up? Let's get rid of that stuff and cut out. I'm really getting nervous. We could get busted, standing here with hot merchandise."

"Stay cool, Lefty," Oscar kept repeating. "I know what I'm doing."

He leaned over and whispered, "Don't you see all these people coming and going? One of them could be a cop! Besides, Antonio's a little shaky right now. I'm sure he's checking us out. You know, if I just walked up and told him I had some stuff, he'd start screaming—to protect himself from the cops."

I cursed those undercover cops again. Would I ever learn to recognize where they might be working?

"Antonio's got a little procedure," Oscar went on. "When most of the customers clear out, that's when Antonio will do business with us. I'm to go over and buy a copy of the New York *Daily News,* fold it, and put the end to my ear. That tells Antonio I have something. He'll walk back to his office. We're to wait for five minutes and then walk back there to him. That'll give him time to check out who's in the store. He has to be cool, man."

Oscar's explanation overcame my jitters somewhat. I realized it was better to have a procedure like this than it would be to rush in—and get busted.

When most of the customers cleared out, Oscar bought the newspaper, folded it, and touched it to his ear. Antonio caught the sign and casually walked back to his office.

Oscar and I looked around for another five minutes. Then he said, "Okay, Lefty; follow me."

It wasn't at all warm yet, but my palms felt sweaty as I wondered whether Antonio had set us up. Who knew what we'd find when we walked into that office? It could be swarming with cops. Antonio could have been pressured by the cops to become an informer—as Jerome had—especially with the way the cops were putting pressure on everyone!

Just before we got to the door, I grabbed Oscar and wheeled him around. "Suppose we open that door and it's swarming with cops?" I whispered. "What then?"

His mouth flew open. "Man, I hadn't even thought about that!" he said. "But you're absolutely right, man. They could have put the heat on Antonio. What do you think we ought to do?"

That was a switch—Oscar asking for my advice!

Well, my first thought was to cut out—that something didn't look right about this deal. But I still had visions of that mountain of heroin, so I said, "Oscar, since you have the goods on you, why don't you go back and stand in the middle of the store? I'll open this door and go in. Now you keep watching the door. If I think it's clear in there, I'll open and close the door, just a little, two times. But so help me, Oscar, if you don't see the signal, you get out of here

quickly. If those cops grab me, they'll have the wrong guy.
I have nothing on me."

"Say, Lefty, you're catching on quick. You'll make a
good partner."

I felt warmed by Oscar's praise and boldly opened the
office door. Antonio sat there behind a wooden table. I noticed a lot of old boxes stacked around—perfect hiding
places for the cops.

"What do you have?" Antonio asked matter-of-factly.

"What do you mean, what do I have? What are you
looking for?"

Antonio blinked. "What are you talking about, kid? I've
never seen you before in all my life. I've dealt with Oscar,
but who are you?"

"The name's Lefty. Mind if I look around?"

As I turned, Antonio picked up a revolver that he must
have had waiting right beside him. Aiming it right at me,
he said in measured tones, "Kid, I'm a busy man. I don't
have time for games. And I've never had anybody treat me
this way before. Now what do you mean, look around?
And your explanation had better be good!"

Now it was my turn to blink in surprise—and to quiver
in fright. I was staring right at the barrel of a loaded gun.
And somehow I knew he wouldn't hesitate to use it.

"Cool it," I said with a lot more bravado than I felt. "I'm
just checking to see whether this place has any cops in it.
Who knows who might be hiding behind those boxes!"

I had heard that Antonio had a short fuse, and I guess I
must have set it off. He jumped up and started kicking
those boxes around, screaming, "Man, you have me all
wrong. There isn't anybody behind those boxes. So tell me
your business, and tell me quickly, or I'll pull this trigger
and then stuff you in one of those boxes and dump it into
the East River!"

"Just cool it," I said again. "Let me signal my partner."

I opened the door twice, and in a moment Oscar walked in. When Antonio saw him, he lowered his gun. "For crying out loud, Oscar," he said, "who is this punk? He's a real amateur. You'd better get rid of him before he gets you into real trouble."

"Oh, come on, Antonio," Oscar said soothingly, "what's the matter? We were just checking things out, that's all."

"Hey, what goes on here?" Antonio demanded. "You do business with me, and I do business with you. I thought we were partners. Now all of a sudden you get suspicious of me. What's up?"

Without answering, Oscar just emptied the credit cards and checks on the table. As the pile got bigger, so did Antonio's eyes!

Then Oscar said, "You'll have to excuse our tactics, Antonio, but my partner and I almost got busted yesterday because of somebody we thought we could trust."

"Ha, that's funny!" Antonio said, laughing.

"What's funny?" I demanded.

"Hey, punk, when I want to talk to you, I'll ring your chimes," Antonio said sarcastically. "You may be a smart one. But I think what you need is for someone to slap you around a little."

I was beginning to realize that Antonio was a lot more bark than he was bite, so I let it go.

"If you guys think you were rocked up a little," Antonio went on, "you ought to hear what's been happening to me! Yesterday two guys came in—kind of shabby looking, you know? I figured they had some business. Well, they started asking questions. Then they reached into their pockets. I thought it was a stickup. But, no, they flashed their badges!"

"You're kidding!" Oscar responded.

"No way," Antonio went on. "Those two were very real cops. They told me they were investigating the problem that this neighborhood is overrun with junkies—and all kinds of stealing and stuff, you know."

I wanted to laugh. Big deal. The neighborhood was overrun with junkies, and there was a lot of stealing. They sure didn't need an investigation to find that out. Everybody knew that.

"Would you believe those cops told me they needed some help in the neighborhood?" Antonio continued. "I guess they were setting up a citizen's committee or something. So what could I tell these guys but, 'You can count on me to help you out.' They went ahead and told me what to be looking for. And I kept nodding my head. And before I realized it, they had appointed me the official spy of the community."

By this time Antonio was laughing so hard he could hardly get the words out. So was Oscar. And this time I knew what they were laughing at and joined them. The whole thing was ridiculous. But I wondered whether those cops didn't suspect what was going on in this store, and this was their way of throwing Antonio off guard! That made me all the more anxious to get our money and get out of there.

Oscar and I counted out the credit cards—fifty of them! Then Antonio tallied the checks on a little calculator.

"I'll give you two thousand dollars for the lot," he announced.

Without a moment's hesitation, Oscar said, "Sold!"

Wow! Two thousand bucks! That would buy us a pretty good supply of the stuff. Maybe not a mountain, but a good-sized hill!

Antonio peeled off twenty hundreds from a large wad he had been carrying in his pocket, and handed them to Oscar. A thousand of that was mine—at least I hoped so.

We shook hands on the deal and Oscar and I hurried away with one thing on our minds: find Spino.

We were so preoccupied that when a voice addressed us from behind, we both about jumped out of our shoes.

"Hey, can I talk to you?" the voice asked.

I saw Oscar's hand go for his gun.

But when we turned around, there stood a mailman.

"Hey, man, what do you want?" Oscar demanded. "You really startled us."

"Sorry," he said as he walked up to us. I kept looking for the bulge under his coat. That would give him away as a decoy cop. But he seemed okay.

He got right to the point. "I understand you guys are dealing in stolen credit cards and checks. Can I work a deal with you?"

After how well—and how easily—our deal had gone with Antonio, I started to say yes. But Oscar exploded. "Listen, doc, what are you talking about? What do you take us for, anyway? We're a couple of honest guys on our way to work. And you come and say something about stolen credit cards. Man, you ought to get thrown in the slammer for fifty years!"

I wanted to protest. Suppose this guy was on the level; he would be a good pipeline for us. I was pretty sure Jerome wouldn't want to do business with us anymore.

"Hey, wait a minute!" the postman responded. "I know all about you two."

"What do you mean, you know all about us?" Oscar demanded.

"I mean, I know all about you from Jerome Atkins."

"Jerome Atkins?" I asked, playing the game. "Who's he?"

"I think it's time to stop playing games," the mailman sneered. "I know who you are. I know what you're up to. I know you just came out of Antonio's, and my bet is that you took credit cards and checks in there and came out with cash. Right?"

Oscar moved close to him and ran his hands on the guy's chest, thighs, and down toward his ankles.

"Okay, man, you're clean," Oscar said. "Now what's your story?"

"First, let me warn you about Jerome," he said. "He's been stealing credit cards for a long time now. But, man, is he stupid! Half the people down there know what he's up to. It won't be long before they nail him. But me, I do it differently."

"Oh?" Oscar interrupted.

"Yes. I work in the back by myself. I'm a supervisor. And I can get all kinds of credit cards and checks—and nobody will ever know about it. I'm safe, man."

"How do we know you're on the level?" I asked. "You could be in with the cops. You know, like an undercover agent?"

He laughed at that. "Listen, you dudes, you don't need to lay that on me. I know where I'm coming from. I need money; you need money; so let's work a deal."

"How did you know to contact us?" I asked.

"Well, to tell you the truth, I heard Jerome talk about you two. Then this morning I decided to take some of my cards and checks to Antonio. I had heard he was the neighborhood fence. I told him I knew what he was up to, but he denied everything, of course. Then he finally said there was a guy I might be able to deal with, and he named you, Oscar. You had just come in, and he pointed you out to me. So I just waited outside until I saw you come out a few minutes ago."

"That dirty Antonio!" Oscar exploded. "He told you who I was?"

The mailman nodded. Then he added, "But don't get mad at him. He explained to me that he had to do it this way, that it was his policy. He said he wouldn't deal with anybody unless he knew them. I guess he's been getting some heat from the cops."

Oscar was still angry. "I ought to go back there and slam that Antonio against the wall," he yelled. "Maybe that would teach him a lesson!"

"Hey, cool it! Cool it!" the mailman urged. "You guys have nothing to worry about from me. I'm the one who should be worried. I'm the one who's pulling those cards and checks from the mail. So let me tell you how we can work a deal."

"What do you have in mind?" Oscar asked.

From one pocket the mailman pulled a bunch of credit cards. From another he pulled out a stack of checks. Oscar snatched them and said, "Don't go away. We'll be right back."

I followed him back into Antonio's and watched as he went through the same procedure. Five minutes later we were back in Antonio's office, and he was staring at some more cards and checks.

"What brings you two back so soon?" he asked. "Did you guys knock off a post office? Or maybe you robbed a mail truck? You haven't been gone more than fifteen minutes. How'd you do it?"

"This business is too good to be true," Oscar replied. "But I want to tell you something, Antonio. I'm really ticked off at you."

"What do you mean, ticked off?" Antonio asked in surprise. "I gave you two thousand dollars in legitimate money. You know me, Oscar; I'm a square dealer. Right?"

"Wrong!" Oscar screamed. "You told a postman who I was!"

"You mean that guy who was in here this morning? Listen, I know that guy. He lives in the neighborhood. He really does work for the post office. He's legit. My problem, Oscar, is that the heat's on. I can't deal directly with a guy like that. So I had to say something."

"You sure did say something!" Oscar yelled. "You ratted on us!"

They stood there glaring at each other. I was realizing that in this business, nobody could be trusted. Jerome turned out to be a rat. So did Antonio. Would there ever come a day when Oscar would rat on me?

I could tell Antonio was getting fed up. "Okay, you two punks," he shouted, "I've had enough out of you. You're calling me a rat? Well, I know who I am, and I know I have to be careful."

"Sure, you have to be careful, Antonio," I said, trying to calm the situation. "But we have to be careful, too."

"Yes," Oscar chimed in, "you're smarter than that, Antonio. Just be careful whose name you give out."

"Don't you punks start giving me advice!" Antonio exploded. "Now get out of here, right now. I don't ever want to see either of you again! Ever! I don't want to do business with you ever again. Do you understand what I'm saying?"

Oscar threw up his hands. "Wait a minute! Wait just a minute!" he said. "It's not that easy!"

Antonio moved back behind his desk and made a move as though he was going for his gun. Quicker than lightning, Oscar had his gun out, aimed right at Antonio. "Don't get any funny ideas, or I'll splatter you against that wall and then I'll rob you. You get your hands up where I can see them!"

Antonio slowly pulled his hands away from his gun and raised them above his head.

"Okay, we don't need to play with these guns," Oscar

said, tucking his gun back in his belt. "You can relax, Antonio. But I want to tell you something, and you get this good. You're always going to deal with me. You'll always deal squarely. You're always going to be open to my business. And if you're not, I'm going to be a rat!"

Oscar wagged his finger right under Antonio's nose. "I'll call those cops, and they'll stake out this place. And then, Antonio, you'll be sent up the river. I mean, Sing Sing, man. And you'll rot in some cell. Do you understand what I'm telling you?"

"You wouldn't do that to me, would you, Oscar?"

"Okay, Antonio, I'll tell you whether I will or not. See these credit cards and checks? What'll you give me for them?"

There were ten credit cards and quite a stack of checks. He tallied them on his calculator and said, "I'll give you one thousand dollars."

Oscar turned to me. "What do you think, partner? Is a thousand bucks enough for all of this?"

A thousand dollars? Was he kidding? We'd already made a thousand each on our previous transaction. I didn't know how we would have to split with the postman. It sounded like a good deal to me, but I figured there must be some reason Oscar was stalling. So I said, "I don't know. Do you think we're getting enough for those checks?"

Antonio glared at me. "Hey, listen. As I told you guys before, I give good deals, and a thousand bucks is a good deal for these."

So I said, "I guess so, Oscar. Let's take it."

"Antonio, we're still in business," Oscar said. "You're no longer a rat, and I'm no longer a rat!"

Antonio smiled and peeled off another ten hundreds. Oscar stuck them in his pocket, and we walked out.

When we got to the street, we turned left. I said, "Hey,

aren't we going the wrong way? The postman is waiting in the other direction, isn't he?"

"Come on, Lefty," Oscar derided me. "Don't tell me you really thought we would go back and split with that turkey!"

"Why not? He's the one who got the cards for us. And he can get some more in the future."

Oscar laughed again. "Listen, man, no way am I going to go back to that guy. He could be an FBI agent, or the cops could have put him up to something—just like they did Jerome. No way. Let's cut out."

"Oscar, you're a genius," I said, almost in reverence. "You are absolutely right. That guy could be an agent. And if he's not an agent, he's not going to go back to the cops and rat on us, is he? He's the one who stole that stuff!"

Oscar slapped me on the back. "Lefty, you're getting really smart. One day they'll put your name in lights with Al Capone. You and he will be the greatest gangsters the world has ever known!"

I laughed. Oscar's praise felt good. But then I thought about Al Capone. He ended up dead!

Well, we headed to find Spino. But when we turned a corner, standing in front of us was the mailman—with a gun aimed right at us!

8

I shot a quick glance toward Oscar, half expecting him to go for his gun. But I guess he knew the mailman would have dropped him in his tracks.

Yet when I glanced back toward the mailman, I noticed

the gun was extended straight out from his body, and his hand was shaking. Obviously he wasn't all that used to using a gun. Maybe this was his first time. But sometimes that could be even more deadly.

Then I thought of that three thousand dollars in cash on Oscar. What rotten luck! After all the hassles with Jerome, Antonio, and this mailman, now we could end up having the money stolen! My dream of that mountain of heroin crumbled.

"Listen, you two," the mailman was saying, "I've been ripped off before, and I smelled something stinky about you. So I followed you. And when you came out of Antonio's and headed in the opposite direction from where I was supposed to be waiting, I ran around the block to head you off. Nobody's going to rip me off again!"

"Hey! Hey! Cool it!" I said. "We were just circling the block to check things out. You have to understand something, and you have to understand it quickly. We didn't know who you were. For all we knew, you could be an undercover cop. We were going around the other way to check and see whether you had some backup men."

"Okay, kid, give me another story!" the mailman snarled. He thrust the gun closer to Oscar and demanded, "Give me my money before I pull this trigger!"

Oscar started to reach for the money. He couldn't give it up that easily. There were two of us and only one of him. I had to stall.

"Listen, sir, so you didn't believe the first story," I said. "But I can prove this. Oscar and I made arrangements for you to deal directly with Antonio. No middlemen."

He laughed contemptuously. "Listen, kid," he said, "there's no sense standing there feeding me all those lies. You two guys thought you were going to rip me off, didn't you?"

I tried to think of something else—anything to avoid giving him that money. But this mailman was smart. And my mind went completely blank.

Then Oscar said, "Hey, man, I know how you feel. Okay, don't believe our stories. That's up to you. But here is the money. Would you believe I got a thousand bucks for those checks and credit cards?"

The guy's eyes brightened. "Really? You got that much?"

"Yeah, man, look here." Oscar reached into his pocket and pulled out the ten hundred-dollar bills and began to count them. The mailman lowered his gun and stepped up close to Oscar.

"Okay, man, I understand we're going to split fifty-fifty. Right?" Oscar asked.

The mailman didn't answer. He simply pushed his gun inside his belt underneath his jacket. Then he extended his hands to take the money.

"Mister, you're dealing with a couple of pros," Oscar said. "I know you don't think much of us, but my partner and I have been in business for a long time. And you can trust us."

Good old Oscar. At least our two thousand dollars was safe. And it looked as though we were going to have five hundred dollars to split as our part of that second sale. My vision of that heroin mountain became clearer.

But as Oscar counted out five of the bills, the mailman jerked out his gun again. "No way!" he shouted. "No way! I want all of it!"

"What?" Oscar demanded. "What do you mean, all of it?"

"I mean, every last penny," he countered. "One thousand dollars!"

"Wait just a minute!" I protested. "We had to put our

lives on the line for that money! I mean, we walked into
Antonio's and made that deal. Without us, you'd have had
no deal at all. So you need us. And you've got to split that
money with us fifty-fifty!"

He wheeled toward me, his gun aimed directly at my
head. "I'm warning you, kid, keep your mouth shut!" he
shouted. "I've heard all I can take from you."

When he saw that that silenced me, he turned toward
Oscar, his gun now aimed at Oscar's head. "Okay, give me
all of it!"

I couldn't imagine Oscar doing what he did. He just simply handed the mailman the entire one thousand dollars—
just like that. No struggle. It seemed entirely out of character for Oscar.

With his free hand, the mailman grabbed the bills and
stuffed them into his pocket. Then he tucked his gun into
his belt again and walked away, chuckling to himself. He
had really outsmarted us and gotten every penny for himself.

As he walked away, Oscar called after him, "Hey, mister
postman, do you know how to pray?"

The mailman glanced back. That's when he saw Oscar's
gun pointed right at him! Now it was our turn to laugh!

We quickly moved the few steps to where the guy stood,
quaking in his boots. "Mister postman," Oscar said, "you
sure are stupid! I mean, you're really stupid. The next time
you hold up a couple of professional criminals, you'd better
check to see if they've got any guns. I mean, man, you are
stupid!"

The startled mailman edged his hands closer to his body.

"Get those hands up!" Oscar screamed.

It didn't take a second command. While Oscar kept him
covered, I walked over, pulled his gun out, and stuck it
under my own belt. I could feel the bulge it made, and it

was fantastic. I had a gun now, and I felt so powerful!

"Okay, Lefty, get our money," Oscar told me.

As I started toward the pocket where he had put the money, the mailman yelled, "Don't you lay a hand on that money, punk!"

When he called me "punk," something broke inside of me. I clenched my fist, reared back, and let that guy have it in the stomach just as hard as I could. He doubled over in pain, and when he did, I came up with my knee square in his face. He reeled backward, blood spurting from his nose. He was howling in agony, but I came down hard with a karate chop that sent him sprawling onto the pavement. As I stood over him, daring him to try anything, I whipped out that new gun of mine and pointed it at his head.

Alarmed, Oscar grabbed my arm, yelling, "Lefty! Lefty! Cool it, man! Cool it! We don't want a murder here on the street!"

Oscar's urgent tone jerked me out of my stupor. I really couldn't believe how violently I had reacted to his calling me a name. Why, I had even cocked the trigger! Another second and that mailman's brains would have been splattered all over the sidewalk!

"I'm sick and tired of people treating me this way," I yelled. "Nobody's going to call me a punk and get away with it!"

"Lefty, so help me, I've never seen you this way before," Oscar said. "What's bugging you, man? You couldn't have gotten that upset over a name!"

I couldn't answer. I really didn't know what it was. But I did know that something down inside me broke loose. And I realized it was something that could get me into big trouble someday.

By this time Oscar himself had pulled the thousand bucks out of the guy's pocket. A crowd was starting to gather, and Oscar called to me. "Let's get out of here, quickly."

After we turned a corner, we slowed to a walk. "I dare that guy to try to come after us," I said. "I'll shoot him with his own gun!"

"You almost did!" Oscar replied. "Lefty, I had no idea you were so mean and ornery. Maybe we ought to knock off a bank!"

I was still furious. People were going to have to treat me with respect. And if they didn't, I'd show them. I carried a gun now. I was going to be a big man on the street. Nobody had better mess with me!

I was so enthralled with my newfound sense of power that I didn't even give another thought to that mailman, who was probably still writhing in agony on the sidewalk. It never even occurred to me that I might have injured him seriously. I just didn't care!

Over at 110th and Madison, Spino was hanging around. Oscar split the money with me fifty-fifty on the way, so we both bought twenty bags from Spino at fifteen dollars a bag. When we each peeled off three hundred dollars, Spino's eyes got really big. It made me feel all the more powerful that I could impress a big-time pusher like him.

Back in our apartment, we immediately got off. In fact, that day we got off five more times! Yes, I was on the mountain of heroin. I had arrived.

That whole week we both stayed high all the time. I was surprised at how fast our money disappeared. Of course, that meant we had to hit the streets again. Sometimes Oscar would go his way, and I'd go mine. Sometimes we'd go together. A lot depended on what we were planning to do.

I was giving my gun a good workout. It really had power.

As soon as people saw it, they'd give me everything they had.

One night I held up an old lady and got one hundred dollars. Right away I went looking for Spino. But that night I couldn't find him. I figured maybe he had gone back to his apartment to get more dope, but I knew I didn't dare go there. Then I got to wondering whether he had gotten busted. That thought brought stark terror. What would I do if Spino got busted?

But just as I felt that panic coming on, a guy walked up behind me and whispered, "Want to buy some dope?"

Startled, I wheeled around and faced a guy I had never seen before in this area.

"What did you say?" I asked.

"I said, do you want to buy some dope?"

Oh, oh! This must be another cop in disguise, because the guy sure didn't look like any dope pusher I knew. He was clean shaven, had rather short hair, and wore a suit and tie. *But wouldn't the cops know better than to disguise someone this way?* I asked myself. Maybe he was in with the cops. Or maybe he was a kid from outside who came down here to buy drugs. Then again, Spino was nowhere around, and I needed to cop. Maybe this guy really did have some drugs to sell.

"What kind of stuff do you have?" I asked, playing it as cool as I could.

"Heroin from Turkey," he whispered. "Man, it's really loaded. And just twenty bucks a bag."

"Let's see it," I said suspiciously. "I usually don't have to pay more than fifteen dollars for good stuff."

"Let me look at your money first," he said.

I eyed him carefully. So help me, I couldn't figure him out. But he was smart. He probably recognized me as a junkie. He knew if he held out some bags, I'd snatch them and run away. In a way, he reminded me of the prostitutes. They always wanted their money first.

But I had the same kind of problem he had. If I held out my money first, he could grab it and run.

Then I remembered. I wasn't at the mercy of those kind of problems anymore! I had a gun now! So I would reach for my money with my right hand and my gun with my left hand. I wouldn't have to pull it—just let him see it. That would keep him from trying anything funny.

"Man, I have plenty of money," I told him. "How much do you want me to show you?"

"How many bags do you want?"

"Oh, maybe five."

"Okay, kid, show me a hundred bucks, and it's a deal."

I slowly pushed back my jacket and exposed the handle of my revolver. He saw it and looked startled. He got the message!

"Hey, man, don't get smart with me!" he warned. "Just reach for your money. You go for your gun, and I'm going to drop you in your tracks."

Then I realized I had automatically put my hand on the handle of my gun. It sure hadn't taken me long to get used to having it!

By this time he had flipped back his suit coat and put his hand up near his chest. I stared. He had a small gun in a shoulder holster!

There wasn't time for fun and games, so I reached into my pocket and pulled out the one hundred dollars I had just robbed from an old lady.

He dropped his hand from his gun and took the money.

"I sure can't figure you out," I said. "Who are you, anyway?"

He laughed—that laugh I had heard policemen laugh. Oh, no! He was a cop.

He moved right up beside me and whispered, "Quick! I'll hand you some dope. Slip it in your pocket and walk about ten feet away and lean up against the building. Then watch what happens."

Before I could ask him what he was talking about, I felt his hand up against my stomach. I quickly grabbed the bags—maybe twenty or thirty of them. I had no way to count them. But I knew it was a lot more dope than I had paid for. What was the deal with this guy?

I quickly slipped the bags into my pockets, and he kind of pushed me away. I moved about ten steps away and leaned against the building, just as he had told me.

Then I heard the roar of a car engine, followed by the screeching of brakes. I glanced in that direction and saw a blue and white car with flashing red lights. The cops!

Two of them jumped out and ran over to the well-dressed fellow I had been doing business with. They shoved him against the building as he screamed, "Cut it out! I don't have anything on me!"

As I watched, they ran their hands all over his body. They even pulled his pockets inside out. When they discovered his gun, they jerked it from its holster.

"Oh, no, you don't!" the guy yelled. "Put it back. I have a permit for it."

"Listen, O'Reilly, we know what you're up to," one of the cops said. "You'd better get out of this neighborhood quickly!"

"Hey, this is a free country," O'Reilly answered. "I came up here to see some of my friends. So why don't you two guys get in your car and do what you're supposed to do? You haven't got anything on me, and you know it."

Just then one of the cops looked over in my direction, and one of them headed over.

Then it hit me. Absolutely dumb, stupid, idiotic. That

was me. I got caught in the setup! O'Reilly wasn't a pusher. He was in with the cops and had set me up. I was standing there with maybe twenty-five bags on me. Those cops were coming over to search me, and O'Reilly was going to flash his badge. I knew I shouldn't have trusted him.

Instinctively I reached for my gun. The cop approaching saw it and had his revolver out while I was still thinking about whether I should pull mine. "Get those hands up!" he ordered.

He didn't have to tell me twice. And he didn't have to draw me a picture. It was all over for me. In New York State you could get life for pushing drugs—and with that much on me, they were going to get me for pushing. And I was sure O'Reilly would tell them I had tried to sell him some drugs.

The cop kept me covered as he asked, "Do you know O'Reilly?"

I blinked. That wasn't the right question—at least, it sure wasn't the one I had expected! I saw O'Reilly out of the corner of my eye, and he was nodding, so I said, "Sure, I know him."

"How come you know O'Reilly?" the cop continued. "Is he your brother or something?" Then he laughed.

"Hey, not so funny," I returned. "O'Reilly's not my brother, but I didn't have a job. My dad is dead, and my mom and little brother didn't have anything to eat. I had to get a hundred bucks, and I knew about O'Reilly. Every so often he comes into the neighborhood and does nice things for the people here. Anyway, I called him and asked to borrow a hundred bucks, and he told me to meet him down here. He's really a great guy. And somebody told me he had a lot of money."

"Part of your story is true," the cop said, still laughing. "O'Reilly's got money. But I've never heard of him giving a penny of it away. He's a greedy, filthy dope pusher."

I glanced over at O'Reilly and pretended to be horrified. "What?" I said. "O'Reilly, a dope pusher? I never would have thought that!"

The cop held his gun near my nose. "Listen, you junkie," he said, "I'll tell you something. We have our eyes on this O'Reilly, and one day we're going to get him, and get him good. I'm warning you, kid, don't be around when we nail him, because somebody's going to get hurt badly!"

"Mr. Policeman, I hear you talking," I responded. "I'll behave myself and stay away from O'Reilly. I had no idea he was a pusher. Oh, wow!"

The cop pushed his gun back into its holster, sort of backed to his car, and got in. His partner followed, and they drove off.

Well, now I was sure of one thing: O'Reilly wasn't an undercover cop. They had me in their grasp. There would have been absolutely no way they would have passed up an opportunity like that to bust me.

O'Reilly walked over to where I was leaning. "Thanks, kid; you saved my life."

"What's with you, anyway?" I demanded. "I thought for sure you were an undercover cop and had set me up by pushing all of that dope into my hands. What's your game, man?"

"Well, you probably won't believe this," he said, laughing, "but I'm a graduate of Harvard Business School. I have a master's degree in business. But I studied the dope market and figured I might as well make some real money. So I made some inquiries, found out where I could get some good dope, and I'm working up some trade. And, man, am I making the money! This beats being the president of some large corporation! I'm just oozing with dough because I've got good stuff. My line from Turkey is reali operating."

My mind was operating, too. I figured maybe I coul make a run for it. After all, I still had O'Reilly's dope. Bu then I remembered his gun. If he were a sharpshooter, tha would be the end of me. I wasn't ready for that.

"Okay," he said, "give me my dope back."

I wasn't about to argue. I looked around to be sure n cops were watching. Then I handed all the bags back to him. "Now give me my five," I said.

"Sure." He handed over the five bags I had paid for "And thanks."

I sure hoped his stuff was good. If it was milk sugar and quinine without any heroin in it, I was coming after thi guy. The cops wouldn't have to worry about O'Reilly, then I'd kill him—just as I'd do to anybody who tried to rip me off.

Somebody must have been watching the transaction, because just as I turned to leave, a voice called, "Hey, what's up?"

I wheeled around, and there stood Spino. I didn't have to answer his question, for he had already buttonholed O'Reilly. "Hey, mister, what's your game?" he demanded

"I don't have any business with you," O'Reilly snarled. "So just keep moving on before you get hurt!"

I gasped. O'Reilly obviously didn't know who he was talking to! Nobody, and I mean nobody, talked to Spino that way!

"Listen, you punk, you'd better have more respect for me!" Spino screamed. "Don't get smart with me, or you'll get hurt badly!"

"Really?" O'Reilly responded. "Mister, who do you think you are, anyway? I said for you to move on before you get hurt. And I'm not afraid of you or anybody else!"

Wow! In a moment there was going to be blood all over the street when these two tangled. I didn't want to be around when that happened, so I started backing away. But not too fast. I was still curious to see what would happen.

"As I told you, punk, don't get smart with me!" Spino shouted. "This is my territory!"

O'Reilly looked at him contemptuously and spit out the words: "You mean it *used* to be your territory. You have competition now, and you might as well get used to it. I've got quality stuff that will—"

O'Reilly never finished that sentence, because Spino leaped like a tiger escaping from its cage and hit O'Reilly full force in the mouth with his fist. O'Reilly staggered from the blow, but grabbed Spino before he fell. They both landed in a heap on the sidewalk, but with Spino on top.

As they fell, I saw O'Reilly go for his gun, so I yelled to warn Spino. He came down hard with his fist and pummeled O'Reilly in the face, and the poor Harvard graduate went limp.

Spino grabbed the gun out of its holster and threw it over to me. He got up and stood over O'Reilly muttering, "I hate competition! I hate competition! What I ought to do is put a bullet in this punk's head!"

"No, Spino! Don't!" I urged. "I think he's on the level."

"Who is he, anyway?" Spino asked me.

"I really don't know. I just met him. He claims he's a Harvard graduate with a degree in business. He said he knew he could make some quick money pushing drugs. That's all I know about him. His name's O'Reilly."

O'Reilly started blinking his eyes and shaking his head back and forth. His eyes focused on Spino, and I saw him start for his gun. What he didn't know yet was that his gun was gone.

He fumbled around for it. Nothing. When he realized

that Spino had taken it, he got to his feet unsteadily. But he still had a lot of spunk in him.

Looking at Spino he yelled, "Mister, maybe you have my gun; but I can get another. And I'm coming back here with my friends. We'll get even. It's going to be all over for you! You hear?"

Spino flipped out his own gun, aimed at O'Reilly, and cocked it. "You listen to me, O'Reilly," he said. "I'm giving you two seconds to get out of this neighborhood. If I ever see you on this street again, I won't ask any questions. I'm just going to kill you. This is my territory, and nobody invades my territory and stays alive. Do you understand me?"

I could tell O'Reilly was shaken by the beating. But he still sneered, "You don't scare me!"

I just couldn't believe this O'Reilly. He was going to get himself killed. I knew Spino wasn't afraid to do it. Knocking off somebody was no big thing to him. I'd heard rumors on the street about how many he'd already killed!

"O'Reilly," I interjected, "you'd better listen to Spino. He's not fooling."

"Neither am I!" O'Reilly answered with a sarcastic laugh. He started dusting off his beautiful suit. He looked so out of place in that suit and tie—especially in the ghetto.

"You'll be back, looking for me," he said pointing at me. "As soon as you put some of that stuff of mine in your veins, you'll know I have the best stuff. And if this creep thinks he's got good stuff, he'll discover it can't compare with mine!"

Spino was enraged. "I said to get out of here!" he screamed. "Now! It's up to me to decide what kind of stuff we have here on this block. And I say, I have the best!"

O'Reilly wasn't about to be bested in any war of words. He was wagging his finger in Spino's face, bragging,

"You're going to hear from me again!" Then he turned and started walking away.

Spino toyed with his gun for a second or two. Then he raised it and aimed. I held my breath. In a minute this argument was going to be settled once and for all.

Two quick shots rang out. O'Reilly crumpled to the ground, screaming and grabbing his legs. Spino could have killed him but chose to shoot him in the legs.

"Believe me, O'Reilly, you won't walk these streets again!" Spino yelled. Then aside to me he said, "He may never walk anywhere again!"

A crowd gathered quickly, and then I heard a siren. The cops!

I took off, and Spino ran right after me. I heard the police car screech to a halt and looked back to see two cops running after us.

"Quick!" I said to Spino. "Follow me!"

I ducked into the next tenement and started up the stairs. But when I looked back, one of the cops was still chasing us!

9

With the cop about a flight behind, I bounded up the steps, Spino at my heels. I had five bags and a gun on me. I had no idea how much Spino had. But neither of us could risk arrest.

Instinctively I reached for my gun. If there was going to be a showdown, I wasn't going to die with a gun in my belt!

I was hitting the steps three at a time when Spino yelled, "Lefty! Help me!"

I hadn't heard any shot, but when I looked around, Spino was holding his right leg and grimacing in pain. "I can't make it!" he called.

"But, Spino, we're almost to the roof! Man, you have to try!"

I grabbed him and helped him, and he struggled to his feet. "I have a bullet in my leg, man," he explained. "It's been there for two years, and when I run too much, my leg gives out."

"This is no time for that!" I told him. I put his arm over my shoulder and lifted. That way he was able to hobble up the few remaining steps to the roof. Out there we could find a place to hide.

But as I hit the exit door and we stepped out onto that flat roof, I realized that this time I was mistaken. There wasn't a place to hide on this roof. Nothing! And running to the next roof was out of the question because of Spino's leg.

"Quick, Lefty, over here!" Spino said. "We have to nail that cop before he nails us."

"No! No!" I shouted. "Don't kill a cop, Spino. Man, they'll hunt you down forever! We'll never get out of the slammer for killing a cop. They may even electrocute us!"

"It's him or me," Spino said with finality. "And no way is it going to be me! Come on!"

He pulled me to the side of the door where the cop couldn't see us. Then we waited.

Those heavy footsteps came closer and closer and closer. Then the door opened slowly. I held my breath.

We watched as the officer edged cautiously onto the roof. I guess he figured we must have taken off running over the rooftops, because he didn't even look in our direction. We both had him covered, and Spino shouted, "Okay, cop, drop it right there!"

I tightened my grip on the trigger. I could see the cop stiffen, but he didn't obey.

He started turning a little toward us. "Two seconds, cop, and tell your wife and kids good-bye!" Spino shouted.

The cop must have turned enough to see our guns glistening in the early-evening moonlight, because the next thing we heard was a loud thud.

"Okay, cop, turn around and face me. And put your arms way up."

When he turned, he said, "You guys aren't going to get away with this one."

"That's not for you to say, cop!" Spino said with a sinister laugh. "Now you just watch that mouth of yours, or we are the last two people you'll ever see! Okay, now, turn back around. No! Keep those hands up high!"

With me covering, Spino walked up behind the cop and ran his hand along the legs of the cop's pants. "Sometimes these cops keep a gun in a holster on their ankles," he explained.

Then Spino pulled out the cop's handcuffs. He spotted a pipe sticking out of the roof, walked over, and handcuffed the cop's wrist to that pipe. "Now sit down and keep your mouth shut!" he ordered.

While this was going on, I walked over and picked up the cop's gun. I couldn't believe my good fortune. Two new guns in one day—and I knew a cop's gun would be the best!

"What are you going to do with that gun?" Spino asked.

"Man, I'm getting weapons so I can put a revolutionary army together and overthrow the government," I said.

"Hey, not so funny. Give me that revolver."

"Oh, Spino. Don't make me give—"

"Hand it over!"

Reluctantly I obeyed. For all my bravado, I wasn't about

to cross Spino on anything. If he said he wanted the gun, I was going to give him the gun.

I couldn't believe what he did next. He limped to the back side of that roof, where the alley was, and dropped the cop's gun over the side. I heard it hit the garbage cans.

I started to protest what a stupid thing that was to do. We could have at least kept the gun and sold it on the street. Somebody would be delighted to get a cop's gun. But Spino seemed so sure that he knew what he was doing.

"Okay, Lefty, we'd better get out of here now," he said softly. "His partner might be along any minute."

He motioned me toward the ridge that separated this tenement from the next one. I followed as he lifted himself across it, obviously in pain. We walked across one roof, then another and another until we finally found an exit and started down the stairs.

I was anxious to get out of there, but Spino was just barely moving because of the pain. Maybe because we were moving slowly, I kept thinking about that gun, wondering whether we would go back and get it.

"Spino," I finally said, "that sure seemed like a stupid thing to do with that gun. It would've been worth a lot on the street."

"Lefty, we've got more to worry about than that gun," he said. "But let me tell you something—something you'd better not ever forget. You can shoot a cop; you can rob a cop; you can hit a cop. But don't ever take a cop's gun."

"Why? Are you afraid it'll misfire?"

"Hey, Lefty, this is serious business." He paused on the steps to be sure I was listening. "You see, a cop's gun is something he has a love affair with. He sleeps with it, eats with it, walks with it, talks with it. Every place he goes, that gun goes with him. A cop knows that sometime he may have to use that gun to save his own life. So if some guy steals that gun, it's like stealing his wife or his kids, or stealing his security."

He started down the steps again. "Man, I've known cops to go after murderers not because they murdered somebody, but because they stole a cop's gun! It's a relentless hunt until the cop catches the guy who stole his gun. And when a cop catches a gun stealer, he doesn't just slip the cuffs on him. Oh, no! I've seen cops really work guys over for stealing their guns. I mean, when they were through, the guys couldn't walk, couldn't see, and couldn't talk! So I mean, man, never steal a cop's gun!"

He glanced back over his shoulder and seemed relieved that nobody was following us.

"Furthermore, Lefty, be sure that cop is watching you when you drop his gun. He's going to start hollering in a couple of minutes, and someone will come to his rescue. But the first thing he'll go for is his gun. Not until he puts that gun back in its holster will he think about chasing us."

By this time we were on the first floor. But instead of sneaking outside, Spino knocked on a door. When a man answered, he announced, "We're building inspectors checking for rats and roaches. Mind if we check your apartment?"

I heard latches clicking on the inside, and the door opened wider. "Come in, come in!" he invited. "I've got lots of both of them, mister inspector. In fact, I've been meaning to call you."

Spino stepped inside and I followed. I had no idea what was going on, but I knew that now was no time to ask questions.

"This will just take a few minutes," Spino assured the man. "Let me check around, and I'll file a quick report. We're getting after the apartment supervisors for not keeping their buildings clean. I'm sure you understand."

As I glanced around, I could see the guy wasn't poor—but he sure wasn't rich, either. Spino wasn't thinking of robbing this guy, was he?

I followed him through the kitchen as he opened drawers. Roaches obligingly scurried to a darkened corner.

Spino moved to the bathroom next. I followed him inside and shut the door. "What's up?" I whispered.

"Not now," he whispered back. "Later."

From the bathroom, Spino headed to the bedroom and checked the man's closet. "These will do," he said aloud to himself.

With that, he headed back to the living room, where the man was still standing. "Sir, you are right," he said, "we did see some roaches—and some evidence of rats. I'll file a report, and we'll do what we can to get this situation cleaned up."

"Oh, thank you, thank you!" the man gushed. "This is a great relief to me. But I didn't know you inspectors worked so late."

Spino laughed. "Well, we have so many rat and roach problems that they put us on two shifts. My partner and I got the swing shift. But we make a living."

Spino had his hand on the doorknob. But then he turned back to the man and said, "Sir, I just happened to notice the clothes in your closet. A friend of mine works for a film company, and he's looking for some good used clothing. They pay a lot of money for it. Well, I noticed you've got a couple of jackets, shirts, and pants there—the kind he is looking for. Do you want to sell them?"

The man blinked in wonderment.

"Tell you what I'll do," Spino said. "I'll give you four hundred dollars for them."

"Four hundred dollars?" the man yelled in surprise. "But, they're not even worth a hundred!"

"I know," Spino returned. "But they just happen to be what my friend is looking for, and he's got to have them by tomorrow morning for this movie he's shooting."

He pulled out a wad of money and peeled off four hundred-dollar bills and held them out.

The man's eyes widened. "You're kidding!"

"No, sir; I've got to have those clothes."

"Mister, for that kind of money, you can have whatever you want."

The three of us headed back to the closet. Spino picked out two shirts, two pair of pants, and two jackets. and tucked them under his arm. Then he handed the four hundred dollars to the man.

When we finally left the apartment, I couldn't wait to ask, "What in the world are you up to?"

"Lefty, you still have a lot to learn. As soon as we hit that street, we'll run into a bunch of cops looking for us. You see, I did a kind of stupid thing up there on the rooftop."

Spino, admit to doing something stupid? That was different.

"Remember when I cuffed that cop to the pipe? Well, when I reached for his handcuffs, I saw his two-way radio. I started to grab it. But just then you picked up his gun. When I saw you stick that gun in your belt, I knew you were going to be hunted for the rest of your life. I had to get that taken care of first. But while I was getting rid of that revolver, I forgot the radio. That means that as soon as we got out of sight, that cop was calling for help. So the street will be swarming with cops, and they'll have our description. So we have to change clothes, right now!"

Spino sure was smart. I hadn't realized the cops would be looking for us that quickly. I thought it wouldn't be until they had found their buddy on the roof. But he could have radioed down our descriptions.

Before we changed, Spino limped back to the same apartment and knocked again. "Do you have two hats?" he asked when the man opened the door. "I'll give you a hundred bucks for two hats."

The guy pulled the bill out of Spino's fingers and announced jubilantly, "I'll be right back."

"What are the hats for?" I asked.

No sooner had I asked, than I knew. We needed those hats to hide our faces.

In moments the guy was back with two hats. "Anything else?"

"No, thanks, sir. That should do it."

We walked down the hallway and made another turn. "Let's hope these aren't too bad a fit," Spino said.

I watched him take off his beautiful suit. What he was putting on was certainly shabby when compared with it. But maybe this would save his life. Me? My clothes were ratty and dirty, anyway. Anything would be an improvement.

Obviously, the clothes didn't fit too well—but then, they weren't too bad, either. We also managed to get everything out of our pockets. I had five bags; Spino must have had thirty—besides that wad of money. Then we put on the hats and pulled them down over our faces.

When we finally got to the front door, we slowly opened it and looked out. Sure enough, down the street red lights flashed off the buildings. So we stepped out of the building and headed the other way.

At the next corner, two cops stood looking up toward the top of a tenement.

"Hey, man, what's going on?" Spino asked.

"A little shooting," one of them answered. "Some pusher got shot in the leg. We think we've got the other two guys cornered up there on that roof." He pointed.

My heart started beating like crazy. If that cop only knew!

"Hope you get him," Spino said as he moved away. "We need to get rid of all the junkies in this neighborhood. They all ought to be shot, if you ask me."

"Well, don't be so hard on the junkies," the cop said. "It's the pushers whom we're really out to get."

"Yeah, man, those are the guys you ought to get," I said.

When we got out of earshot, Spino started to laugh.

"What's so funny?" I demanded.

"Well, no sooner did I mention junkies than you had to jump in and pick on the pushers," Spino said. "But I guess that's only fair, isn't it?"

Spino was limping again now. "I have to get off my feet," he said. He spotted an empty taxi heading our way, hailed it, and we got in.

"Fifty-second and Park Avenue," he told the driver.

Why were we going there? That was where the rich people lived, and we looked like a couple of bums. But I was learning to wait and see.

When we got to Fifty-second Street, Spino told the driver, "Right over there. Just take a left here and drive down half a block."

The cab pulled up at what looked like the entrance to an expensive apartment building. A doorman even appeared to open the cab door with a "Good evening, Mr. Reynolds. How are you this evening?"

Spino, using an alias?

"Just fine, Mr. Jepson," Spino said as he got out of the cab. "And I'd like you to meet a friend of mine, Alex Kerris."

I didn't know whether I liked my new name or not, but I figured I'd better remember it.

While I was shaking hands with the doorman, Spino paid the driver. Mr. Jepson opened the door for us, and we walked in on thick, plush carpeting under a huge chandelier that hung in the foyer. The walls were lined with expensive paintings. What was Spino doing here?

He didn't tell me. He simply led the way to the elevator, and we rode up to the fifteenth floor. No one else was in there, so I asked, "What gives?"

"Later."

When we got off the elevator, he led me into a fabulous apartment—gorgeous furniture, grand piano, and a window that overlooked the Hudson River. I could see the lights along it. Everything looked spectacular from this height.

Again I asked, "What gives?"

"Lefty, this is my apartment—my real home," Spino said. "The other place is where I keep my bodyguards and where I stash my stuff. Now don't get any ideas. My stuff is always guarded—and guarded well. But I make good money, and I like to live high. So I rent this elaborate apartment. Now, so help me, Lefty, I never bring any of my friends up here—except maybe a girl now and then. But I didn't know what to do with you back there in the ghetto. And I did owe you something for helping me. You probably saved my life. So I decided to bring you here with me to spend the night. But I want you to get something straight. So help me, if I ever see you hanging out here or coming around here without an invitation from me personally, I'll kill you—just as I'll kill you if you come to my apartment in the ghetto. Whenever we meet, it has to be on the street."

I nodded. No way would I double-cross Spino. And I couldn't help but be impressed at the attention I was getting.

"I have to get off, Spino," I said.

"I understand," he replied, leading me to a spare bedroom. "This is yours for the night. But don't expect me to join you in your drugs. I have to keep my wits about me. I can't afford to take dope."

That should have told me something about pushers, but I was hooked. No lecture would get me off drugs.

That night at Spino's apartment was like heaven. I got off, then I crawled into that plush bed. I'd never known such luxury.

I got off again the next morning. Spino didn't seem to be in a hurry to get back to the ghetto—and I sure wasn't, either.

Late that afternoon a buzzer sounded. Startled, I jumped. "What's that? What's that?"

"Oh, that's just the front-door buzzer," Spino replied. "Could be the maid or one of my friends."

I tagged along as he headed for the door. He looked through the little two-way glass. "Hey, it's a delivery man with a package," he said. "Probably from one of my girl friends."

As Spino unlatched and opened the door, the delivery man said, "A package for you, sir."

Spino reached for it, but the man said, "If you don't mind, may I come inside? You'll have to sign this receipt that you've received the package."

When Spino opened the door wide, I gasped. I went for my gun, aiming it at the delivery man's head.

"Drop it!" Spino ordered. "I told you not to try anything funny around my apartment. You're not going to try to rip off—"

"Alonzo, get your hands up," I ordered, ignoring Spino, "or I'll splatter your brains all over that wall."

The package clattered to the floor as Alonzo's hands went up.

Spino spun around and tried to grab my gun. "He's no delivery man, Spino!" I yelled. "He's a junkie!"

When he heard "junkie," Spino flicked his gun out and aimed it at Alonzo.

"Are you on the level, man?" he demanded.

"Man, I don't know anything about any junkies," Alonzo responded. "And I don't know anything about any Alonzo. My name's Ray Stark, and I'm just a delivery man."

"I'll show you who he is," I told Spino.

I grabbed Alonzo, pulled him inside the apartment, and slammed the door. Then I spun him around and shouted, "Spread-eagle, man; one false move, and it'll be your last!"

From Alonzo's back pocket I pulled a switchblade. "This is the first sign, Spino. Most junkies carry switchblades."

I grabbed Alonzo's arm, shoved it behind him, and pushed up his sleeve. "Lesson number two, Spino; look at this track."

He nodded. "Now, Spino, check the package."

He picked it up and tore the wrapping off. Inside was a dirty, old, block of wood.

Spino sprung into action—the way he had against O'Reilly. He doubled his fist and hit Alonzo in the back of the head, slamming his face into the wall. As Alonzo's knees buckled, Spino shouted, "I'll kill you! I'll kill you! I'll kill you!"

Alonzo tumbled to the floor, and Spino started kicking him unmercifully.

"Easy, Spino, easy," I cautioned. "Don't kill him here, whatever you do, or we'll never get out of this one."

That calmed him for the moment.

"What were you doing here, Alonzo?" he demanded.

"I can answer that," I said. "He came here to rob your apartment. He evidently ripped this uniform off somewhere. Right, Alonzo?"

He didn't respond. I grabbed his shirt and pulled him to his feet. Throwing him back against the wall, I demanded, "Isn't that right, Alonzo?"

"You'd better talk!" Spino screamed.

Alonzo shook his head around. "Okay, okay, cool it!" he said. "I admit I know Lefty. But I don't know who you are. I had heard that someone rich lived here, so I came looking for a place to rob. I was looking for stuff like jewels and gold. So help me, that's the truth!"

"Do you think he's telling the truth, Lefty?" Spino asked.

"Yes, I think so."

"Okay, Alonzo, you can take your package and get out," Spino said. "I really ought to kill you. But Lefty's right; there would be no place to hide your body. So you get out of here quickly. And so help me, if I ever again see you within five hundred feet of this apartment house, I won't ask for any explanations. I'll kill you on the spot. Do you understand?"

Alonzo grabbed the box and scooted out the door. Spino slammed the door after him and latched it.

"Lefty, how do you think he knew to come to this apartment?" Spino asked. "You didn't call him, did you? You don't suppose it's out in the ghetto where I live, do you?"

"Hey, man, one question at a time," I responded. "I haven't touched your telephone. I appreciate the favor you did for me in letting me come up here, and I'm not about to mess around with you. Frankly, Spino, I think it was just chance that he came here."

As we walked back into the living room, Spino said, "Let me pour you a drink. I need something to calm my nerves. Then in a little while we can drive back over to—"

The ringing of the phone interrupted his sentence. He answered and kept saying, "Yes, yes, yes." Then he hung up.

"It's the cops," he said. "They want to come up and talk to me about Alonzo. They caught him on his way out of the building."

I leaped off the sofa. "I have to get out of here, now!" I said. "No way am I going to be around here to talk to any cops!"

"Alonzo must have told them what apartment he came to," Spino went on. "I told them yes, he had been here."

"That was dumb, Spino. Why didn't you lie?"

"Listen, Lefty, I have to put on the other side of my face when I'm here," Spino explained. "Here I'm not a drug pusher. I'm a law-abiding citizen. I'm out to uphold justice, so I'm going to help them nail this guy, and nail him good."

"I have to get out of here, now!" I said in panic. "Suppose Alonzo ratted on me? Suppose he told them I was a junkie? That wouldn't go well for you, either. I have to get lost."

"You're right, man," Spino answered. "Take the elevator to the first floor. When you step out, take a left, then another left. That's the rear entrance. Don't go out the front. It's probably swarming with cops."

I was halfway out the door when he finished giving me directions. An elevator came quickly. At the first floor I followed the easy directions and in a moment was out on the street.

I turned left to go toward Park Avenue. Up ahead were bright, flashing, red lights. The street was blocked.

I headed the other way. Oh, no! The other end of the block was closed, too. I was trapped! Now what?

For a moment I stood there, puzzled. Then a van came through the police barricades and moved slowly toward

me. Big red letters showed up strongly on the white van:
PENNYINGTON'S TV SALES AND SERVICE.

Just a few steps away the van stopped, and two guys in
coveralls got out. A plan began forming in my mind.

I reached toward my belt and felt my revolver. Then I
headed toward the two TV repairmen—and my passport to
freedom.

10

I had to get through that barricade at the end of the
street—and I was beginning to formulate my plan. Knowing my gun was ready, I walked up to the two TV repairmen and asked, "Isn't it rather late in the day for you two
men to be working?"

"Yes, it sure is," one of them said disgustedly as he
looked in my direction. "We have this last TV set to deliver, and then—"

"Who's the set for?" I asked, trying to look as serious as I
possibly could.

The other man paused, reached for his clipboard, looked
at it, and said, "Mrs. Ada Wilkins."

"Oh, no!" I said, bursting out in tears. I threw myself on
one guy's shoulder.

"Hey, son, what's the matter?" he asked with great concern.

I never was much of an actor, but I could almost always
turn on the tears. It had usually worked with my mother.
So it wasn't much effort to keep sobbing and then finally
choke out the words, "Mrs. Ada Wilkins was my mother."

I guess one guy didn't hear my "was," for he slapped me on the back and said, "Young man, cheer up! You'll be able to watch TV in style. I mean, this set is the best in the house. It has locked-in color and remote control. It's the biggest picture we have. And, I might say, the most expensive."

I kept sobbing as I said, "Sir, I don't want the TV."

"What? You don't want this TV set? Your mother certainly wanted it!"

"Sir," I said, wiping the tears from my eyes and trying to act brave, "my mother died last night."

You should have seen their mouths drop open! "Oh, no!" one of them said. "I am so sorry. And to think I talked to her last week when she came to the store. She seemed so healthy and so happy."

"Yes, I know," I answered. "I guess that's why it's such a great shock. One minute Mom was laughing and having a great time with us. The next minute she was on the floor— dead."

"How did it happen, son?"

I really had a great story going, so I decided to lay it on thick. After all, if I was supposed to live in this ritzy neighborhood, my story had to match.

"Well," I began, "she had fixed a beautiful, delicious dinner—steak and all the trimmings. And even now it seems kind of strange. Mom really put on a spread last night. I mean, she went way overboard—champagne, caviar, the whole bit. After dinner she came into the living room and told us how happy she was about the new TV set, that it probably would be coming today. Then she smiled at me and, just like that, her knees buckled and she hit the floor—dead."

I reached for the man and started sobbing again. He put

his arm around me and gently patted my back. "Son, don't cry. Don't cry. I'm sure somehow everything will turn out all right."

I looked at the box containing that huge TV set. If only my story were true. Would I ever love to have that set!

"And to think Mom won't be here to enjoy that TV set that she wanted so badly," I continued.

"Well, she paid cash for it," the man said as he looked at his clipboard. "We have to deliver it. At least you'll be able to enjoy it."

"Oh, no!" I said. "Please don't do that. Every time I looked at that set, I'd think of my mother. I'm sure you understand."

The man nodded. "But we can't take it back," he said, "because it's paid for. Are you sure somebody else in the family won't want it?"

"I'm the only one left now," I said, "and I really don't know what I'm going to do. I'm sure there's enough insurance so that I can go to college and all, but I just can't stand the idea of having that TV set in my apartment. Please take it back. Maybe you know some family who needs a nice TV set. Maybe one of you might want to have it."

I could see greedy smiles flick across their faces and knew what was going on in their minds. Of course they'd like to have that TV set—to sell, if nothing else. They were planning to drop it off somewhere; but were they going to be in for a big surprise!

As they pushed the big box back inside the van, I asked, "If you gentlemen don't mind, I'd sure like to have just a peek at that set. I do have a lot of fond memories of my mother. Is it okay if I just take a look?"

"Sure!" they echoed in unison and motioned me to follow them inside the van.

As both of them reached down into the box, I whipped out my revolver. "Okay, men, do exactly as I say, and nobody will get hurt."

As they turned and saw the gun, their eyes bugged out. "Get your hands above your heads," I ordered.

It was cramped inside the van, but they shot their hands up where I could see them and where I was sure they wouldn't be trying anything funny.

"Hey, son, listen, take it easy, will you?" one of them said. "I mean, we understand how upset you must be over your mother's death and all that, but don't take it out on us! We didn't have anything to do with it. I mean, we're really sorry for you, but there isn't much else we can do."

"Don't feel sorry for my mother," I said derisively. "After all, she's dead. You'd better feel sorry for yourselves. One false move and I'll splatter your guts all over this van!"

The younger of the two guys started to quiver. "Mister, please don't hurt me!" he begged. "I have a wife and kids at home."

"Shut up!" I yelled. "You start squealing like a stuck pig, and you'll be the first to go!"

His mouth snapped shut. I knew I had both of them scared to death. I didn't think they'd try anything smart—even though the cops were just down at the end of the block.

"Okay, both of you up front, real naturallike," I said. "You've made your last delivery, and you're headed back to the shop. And I'm going to lie here on the floor with my gun pointed at your heads. You're going to drive through that police barricade up ahead as though nothing had happened. If a cop gets smart and asks about the TV set you were supposed to deliver, you just tell him the lady wasn't home, and your company won't let you deliver a set unless there's somebody there to sign for it. And you'd better make it believable, because I'm going to tell you something. I just got through doing time in prison, and I'm not going back there. I'll kill, or I'll get killed, but I'm not going back. Do you understand?"

Both nodded vigorously.

Keeping my gun trained on the two, I reached around and slammed the rear door. Then I motioned them into the front seat. I spread out on the floor.

Tires squealed as we took off. "Hey, take it easy!" I yelled. "Don't look suspicious, or there's going to be trouble; I mean, real trouble. I never have to shoot twice. The first shot drops them in their tracks. And your bodies will look horrible splattered against that windshield!"

The driver stuttered something about being scared, but I yelled, "Shut up and drive!"

The van slowed as we neared the barricade. Even from my position in back I could see the reflection of flashing red lights. I held my breath, tightening my grip on the trigger. If the cops stopped us, would I really have guts enough to pull the trigger?

Suddenly the van picked up speed again. The driver called back, "Relax, man. The cops just waved us through."

When we were a couple of blocks down the street, I got up on my knees and announced, "Okay, we're going to drive over to the Brooklyn docks. It's nice and desolate over there."

The man sitting on the passenger's side turned around and pleaded, "Please mister, don't kill us and throw us in the river. I've heard about guys like you. Please be merciful."

"What do you mean, you've heard about me?" I demanded. "You don't know me."

"Listen, when you pulled that gun on us, I knew what we were up against. You're a drug addict. I know. My brother is on drugs. I know you want money. Well, mister, I'm going to stand up, and you can reach into my back pocket and take my wallet, money, credit cards, everything. And my partner here—you can take his, too. Take all you want; just don't kill us. Okay?"

"Hey, those wallets—that's a good idea," I said, acting as if that hadn't even occurred to me. "Why don't we do that now?"

The man started off his seat. "Just a minute!" I shouted. "Not so fast! How do I know you don't have a gun. You just lift yourself up gently, and I'll pull your wallet."

He gingerly lifted himself up, and I grabbed his wallet. One glance inside told me it had plenty of money in it. This was a nice bonus from my plan. I stuck the wallet into my pocket and turned toward the driver.

"Mister, just keep driving," I said, "but lift yourself gently off that seat. One false move, and it's all over."

He obeyed, and I grabbed his wallet, too. It was almost too easy.

"Thank you very much, gentlemen," I said, "but we are still going over to the Brooklyn docks."

"What?" the driver yelled. "We got you through the police barricade. You robbed us. Please, mister, please don't kill us!"

"What's the matter? Are you afraid to die?"

"Yes, I'm afraid to die. This may sound stupid, but why don't you let me live? I'll earn some more money. Then you can come and take my money the second time. If I'm dead, you won't be able to rob me again."

I muffled a laugh. It was kind of a cute answer. But I still had other things in mind, and I couldn't do them here. I needed a desolate spot. It was starting to get dark, and I knew it was unlikely anyone would be over by the docks.

"Go down the East Side Highway and take the Brooklyn Bridge," I ordered.

Both of them sat there staring ahead in stony silence. After we crossed the bridge, I directed them down along the docks. It was deserted and gloomy—really spooky down there.

"Okay, slow down," I said. "Let me take a look here."

I studied the long row of docks. When I spotted a dilapidated one, I said, "Okay, turn right and drive slowly toward the end."

Good! It was deserted—just what I had hoped for.

When we were almost to the end of the dock, I said, "Okay, stop here."

Both wheeled around and looked at me. In the gathering darkness I could see that their faces were ashen white with fear. They knew this was the moment of truth.

Both of them started pleading and screaming, "Don't kill us! Don't kill us!"

"You do as I say!" I ordered, ignoring their pleas. "And don't try to run for it. I mean, I was a sharpshooter in the marines. I can knock a guy off at five hundred yards, so don't try to run!"

"Okay, okay," the driver responded. "Whatever you say, mister, we'll do it. You won't have any problem from us."

"First, we have to get out of this van," I said. "We're all going out the rear door."

I edged myself in that direction, carefully keeping my gun aimed at them as they got out of their seats and moved toward me. I pushed the door open and jumped to the dock. They followed.

"All right, take off those uniforms."

They unzipped their coveralls and stepped out of them.

"Now throw them over to me. Gently."

The guy about my size threw his first, so I caught it and let the other one fall at my feet. It was a chore, keeping those guys covered while I slipped on those coveralls. But I managed—mostly, I think, because they were too terrified to try anything.

The extra weight of the coveralls felt good against the chill of the evening. I strutted around a little, thinking how good I looked in a uniform. "Hey, I should have been in the TV business," I said. I tossed the other pair of coveralls into the back of the van.

They laughed nervously, and one of them said, "Yes, sir."

"Now take off all your clothes," I ordered.

"Everything?"

"Every last bit, including your shoes!"

When they hesitated, I cocked my gun. That started them peeling off things in a hurry. I had them throw everything into a pile near the edge of the dock; then I kicked all their clothes and shoes into the river.

I had to catch myself to keep from laughing. They looked so ridiculous standing there trying to cover their nakedness. I knew it must have embarrassed them terribly, but I still had to keep them terrified, and I decided this was a good way to do it.

"See those clothes of yours?" I asked. "They went to the bottom of those cold, dark waters. And if you don't do as I say, that's what's going to happen to you. Understand?"

They nodded.

"Now here's what I'm going to do. I'm going to drive away in your van, and you guys will stand here and wait exactly one hour. Do you understand that? One hour. Then you can go. But if you go squealing to the cops about this, it's all over for both of you. You can tell your boss that you don't know what I look like, you don't know where I went, you don't know where I left you, and you don't remember anything. Is that clear?"

Their teeth were chattering, but they didn't answer me.

"I said, do you understand?" I yelled. "Or do you want me just to shoot you now and throw you into the river?"

There was no further hesitation. The driver, who seemed to be the leader of the two, said, "Mister, we fully understand. We don't have any idea what happened. We're in a complete daze. We don't know what happened to our clothes or our wallets. We don't know what happened to the TV set or the van. We don't know anything. Right, Morris?"

"Right!" Morris responded.

"That's better!" I said. "I don't know why I'm not finishing you two off right now. You can thank heaven for mercy!"

I slammed the rear door of the van and ordered the two of them to move up in front of the van. "You stand there while I back out of here," I said. "One false move, and I'll let you have it. I guess you've noticed that I'm left-handed, so it's not going to be any problem for me to hold this gun out the window and aim it right at you."

Drive the van? I hadn't driven anything since I learned how at my uncle's farm a year ago. Would I still know how? Well, it was a little late to worry about that now. I had to get out of this mess somehow.

I got the van started, shoved it into reverse, and slowly backed away. I'll admit I wasn't very smooth in handling it, but I was getting away.

The guys stood right where I told them to stand and made no effort to move, so I laid the gun on the seat beside me—it would be ready, in case.

As I got back to the sidewalk and started to turn the wheel to go onto the street, someone banged on the side window. There stood a night watchman.

"Hey, what's going on?" he demanded. "What's a TV repair truck doing down here this time of evening?"

Oh, oh! I had to think of something.

I gingerly reached for my revolver. This old man would be no match for me in a shoot-out. But I kept hoping I wouldn't need to go for my gun.

"Well, hello there," I said, stalling for time. "Is there some problem with my being down here this time of evening?"

"There sure is! What are you doing on this dock?"

I laughed. "Mister, if I told you, you'd never believe me."

"Try me."

"Okay. My buddies and I were having a little drink together. I mean, we weren't drunk or anything, and we got to kidding about coming down to this dock and taking a swim in the East River. Well, I told them I thought they were crazy and wouldn't do it. So we made a bet. We each laid twenty dollars down. Well, I chickened out. But if you'll look down at the end of the dock, you'll see my buddies ready to dive into the river. Look right down there, mister."

I pointed, and the watchman peered toward the end of the dock. The two guys still stood there.

"They're completely naked and ready to jump in," I told him.

"What? We can't allow that!" he shouted. He took off running in the direction of the two TV repairmen. I backed into the street and took off.

I drove up the ramp to the Brooklyn Bridge and headed back to my old neighborhood. I had pulled off a big heist, and I was full of all sorts of ideas of what I was going to do now. Of course, I could pawn the TV set. And I could pawn the truck. But before I did that, I could become a TV repairman.

I looked down at the name on my coveralls. Arnie. That was my name now. Arnie, from Pennyington's TV Sales and Service. It made me feel important.

Up at 110th and Madison I saw Oscar leaning up against a building. I pulled up alongside and yelled, "Hey, Oscar, want to buy a TV set?"

He squinted at me, trying to figure all this out. Then, still looking terribly puzzled, he walked over to the van.

"Oscar, it's me. Lefty."

His mouth flew open. "Hey, Lefty, where have you been? I was worried when you didn't come home last night. What's with this van? Did you get a job?"

"Yeah, man, I decided to go straight. I am now working for Pennyington's. Would you believe I made my first sale and am on my way to deliver it now? Want to come along?"

Oscar didn't have to be invited twice. He jumped in, saying, "Soon as you deliver it, I'm going to steal it."

"Come on, Oscar, as I told you, I've gone straight."

"Uh-huh," he grunted. "And I suppose you changed your name to Arnie, too."

Nuts! There was no fooling Oscar.

"Come on, Lefty, level with me. Where'd you get this rig?"

"It's a long story, Oscar, and I won't bore you with all the details. Let's just say I got it from two TV repairmen. And they threw in a huge TV set with the deal. You should see it; it's absolutely fantastic!"

I slid out of the driver's seat and moved back by the big

box. "Look here," I said, tearing down a corner of the box.

"Wow!" Oscar exclaimed. "That's got to be the biggest TV set I've ever seen!"

"You'd better believe it. They told me it was the top of the line. Who's the best fence around? Let's see what we can get for it."

"Antonio's closed by now," Oscar said, looking at his watch. "But I heard about a new operation. A couple of guys on the street said the guy really gives good prices. His name is Abe Steinman. And he's smart enough to stay open late—to accommodate our business. If you deal with him, you don't have to stash stuff somewhere all night."

"Sounds great!" I said. "Why don't we drive over and see him?"

"He's over on Ninety-sixth Street," Oscar told me.

A few minutes later we drove up in front of what looked like a second-hand store. "You wait here," Oscar said. "Let me check this out."

I waited nervously as Oscar went inside. But in a few minutes he was back announcing, "The guy's on the level, Lefty. He's really interested in TV sets. In fact, he said he'd rather have them than anything. They're easier to move."

A big guy followed Oscar out of the store. I noticed his expensive suit and alligator shoes. He had loads of jewelry around his neck and at least six rings on. Business must be good.

When I showed him the set, his eyes bugged. "And you say it's brand-new?" he asked excitedly. "I have a customer who's been asking, 'Abe, when are you going to get me that TV set?' I can move this one right away. How much you want for it?"

That was different. Fences usually told you how much they'd give you.

When I didn't respond, Oscar said, "Three hundred bucks."

"Sold!" Abe called excitedly.

Oscar and I lugged the set into the store. I noticed he had a lot of other goods around—all stolen, probably.

Abe's office seemed almost too nice for a fencing operation—especially its plush carpeting, big oak desk, and pictures. Gorgeous framed ones of beautiful, naked girls. And I also noticed a well-stocked wet bar.

Abe pulled a cash box out of the bottom drawer of the desk, reached inside, and pulled out three hundred-dollar bills. He started to hand them to Oscar, but I grabbed them. "I'll take those," I said. Oscar said nothing.

"Listen, young man, I really need good TV sets. Do you have any more around?"

"Sure, Abe. How many do you need?"

"If they're like that, I can use as many as you can bring. And I'll give you top dollar for them."

I had a TV repairman's coveralls and a TV repair van. Now I had a fence who would buy all the sets I brought him. This was going to be almost too easy.

When we got outside and jumped into the van, I said, "Oscar, how would you like to go into business with me?"

"How's that?"

"Well, you are going to be employed by my company as a TV repairman. I mean, you and I are in business."

"Lefty," he protested, "I don't know anything about repairing TV sets. I hardly know which button to use to turn one on."

"Oscar, you just do as I say, and I'll split the profit with you fifty-fifty. Okay?"

We drove back toward our neighborhood, parked the TV van in a relatively safe but secluded spot, and headed back to our apartment. I brought the extra pair of coveralls inside with me, and then we went out looking for Spino.

He was back in his usual spot. I made no mention of having spent the night in his plush apartment. He just acted as though he hadn't seen me in a couple of days.

Oscar and I came back to our apartment and got off.

The next day I had Oscar try on the other pair of coveralls. They were a little big on him, but not too bad.

"Now remember, Oscar, you're Morris and I'm Arnie. Okay?"

"Morris? Sounds like a name for a cat on TV," Oscar said.

After a good laugh at his cleverness, I said, "Okay, we have to go out and repair some TV sets."

Oscar trotted along after me toward the van. It was a little different for me to be calling the shots—but it felt good.

We drove down Madison looking for a phone booth. When I found one, I said, "Come with me."

In the booth I began to run my fingers down a page. "Let me see," I said, "I want to find somebody in the Seventies. Real rich people."

"What are you doing?" Oscar demanded.

"Come on, Oscar. I used to follow you. Now you need to learn to follow me. We're going to make some big money. I mean, really big money, man!"

As I ran my finger down the listings, I spotted one at an address on East Seventy-sixth Street: Thelma Avedon. Even the name sounded rich.

I deposited the coins and dialed the number, hoping there would be no answer. The phone kept ringing and ringing.

"Lefty, for crying out loud, let me in there," Oscar called. "I don't know what's going on."

I paid no attention. I let the phone ring and ring. Still no answer. That was exactly what I wanted.

"Okay, Oscar, you and I are in for some really big money. "Not only TV sets, but jewelry and all kinds of valuables. I mean, we are really going to make a haul, man!"

"Lefty, this had better be good," Oscar said flatly. "You get me busted, and I'll kill you, man."

"No way, Oscar; no way!"

I headed for the van, smiling and congratulating myself on the cleverness of my latest plan. We were about to make a bundle.

"Let's head for Thelma's house," I said as we headed back into the traffic. "Is she going to be surprised!"

11

Oscar looked at me warily as we drove along in the TV van. "Lefty, you'd better know what you're doing," he said. "We've been getting away with a lot of things lately. That worries me. Our number is just about up, and one of these times we're going to get busted."

I started to feel nervous when Oscar said that. What if this caper didn't work? What if Morris and Arnie squealed to the cops? The cops wouldn't have much trouble spotting a white van with those huge red letters on it. So help me, if I heard a siren, I was going to run for it!

We drove a couple of blocks without saying anything else. Then I heard it—a siren. I glanced into the side mirror and could see a police car right behind me, red light flashing.

"Hang on, Oscar!" I shouted as I tromped on the accelerator.

"Lefty, I knew you'd do it! I knew you'd do it!" Oscar kept repeating. "It's all over now!"

At the intersection just ahead the light turned red. Cars, hearing the siren, were pulling to the side. Pedestrians were turning to watch. There was no way I could stop for that light. All I could do was to lay on the horn and hope for the best. If a car was coming across, this was going to be it.

I floored the accelerator, and Oscar grabbed the dashboard, preparing for the inevitable crash.

But it looked as though we were going to make it. Then I heard tires screech. Off to my left I could see a car sliding toward us. I couldn't see how we were ever going to get out of this one!

But, miraculously, when the other car slid, it banged the curb and bounced into a parked car. We made it through.

I thought maybe the cops would stop for the accident, but they kept coming after us. I whipped to the right at the next intersection. They did, too.

I kept on the horn because I sure didn't want to hit some pedestrian. And I kept pushing that accelerator. If I could get far enough ahead of those cops, maybe I could shake them.

I made a quick right and then another. The siren was getting fainter now. They must have missed the last turn. I slowed down and wiped the beads of perspiration off my forehead. Oscar had his hand over his heart.

"Lefty," he said, "all I could see was prison bars. Man, I didn't know you could drive that way! I've never seen anything like it in my life!"

I was too scared to accept the compliment. Shaking all over, I pulled to the curb. I didn't know I could drive that way, either!

As I opened the door, Oscar said, "Where you going now?"

"I've had it with this TV repair business," I replied. "We're hot, man. We're going to get it and get it good. I really thought I had a great idea, but I'm afraid it's going to get us busted."

"You get back in here!" Oscar ordered. "You said if I came along, we were going to make a lot of money. Well, I'm holding you to that, man. Let me tell you, I have to get some money quickly or I'm going to start getting sick. Now why don't we just do this thing you were planning and do it really quicklike. I've got to have some money."

"Oscar, I told you, we're hot!" I protested. "I mean, really hot. Let's just take off these coveralls and walk down the street. We'll find somebody to mug or something."

"What kind of a friend are you?" Oscar screamed. "I took you along with me when you were sick. I even risked my life for you. I've taught you everything you've learned so far. Now I've got a pretty good idea what you're up to, and I think it will work. Let's do it quickly. I have to have some money. Now!"

As we sat there arguing back and forth, I glanced in the rearview mirror. Oh, no! A police car was heading toward us.

"Oscar, are you ready to run? Look back there."

He wheeled around and cussed. "Don't run," he said. "We'll get shot in the back, and they'll call it self-defense."

Sure enough, the car pulled up behind the van, and two cops got out. As they approached, I could see their hands were held close to their revolvers. They didn't know it, but my hand was on my gun, and Oscar's was on his!

"Do you have any identification?" the officers asked me.

"What's the matter, officer? We didn't break any law."

"I didn't say anything about breaking the law," he responded. "But we've had a report about a stolen van, and one of our patrol cars was just pursuing one and lost it. You wouldn't know anything about that, would you?"

"What?" I responded. "Don't tell me they found that stolen van already? My boss said it was stolen last night. We heard about it when we came to work this morning. You think you've found it?"

"No, we're not positive," the cop said. "But we thought maybe one of our cars had it in pursuit. They evidently lost it in the area."

"Oh, wow!" I exclaimed. "Hang on just a minute. My boss is in that apartment building there. Let me go get him. Maybe we should go with you and identify that van."

Without waiting for an answer, I slipped out of the van and headed up the steps of a nearby apartment building. My agile mind had just come up with an idea!

When I got to the apartment door, I turned around and called, "Hang on just a minute. My boss is going to be happy about this news!"

Poor Oscar. I knew he figured I was deserting him. But I certainly couldn't explain my plan to those two cops!

Inside the apartment house, I knocked on the first door on my right. A man answered.

"Sir, I'm from the Pennyington TV Repair Company, and there's been a shoot-out down the street. I've got to call the police."

The man peered out, saw my uniform, and quickly un-latched the door. I pushed inside, asking breathlessly, "Where's the phone?"

He pointed to the next room, and I ran to it and dialed 911—the emergency number.

When a woman answered, I said, "Send help, quickly! A policeman has been shot!"

I couldn't remember what street we were on, so I called to the man, "What's your address?"

"Two thirty-nine East Eighty-fifth."

I told the dispatcher, "The shooting took place on Eighty-second Street near Second Avenue. There's a police car right out in front of Two Hundred Thirty-nine East Eighty-fifth. Radio them. They're not very far away."

"Will do immediately," the dispatcher said.

I hung up the phone and waited. The man, looking agitated, said, "Seems as though cops are being killed every day. It's just terrible. I mean, terrible."

"Yes," I answered. "I sure hope they catch the guy."

"You say there's a car right out front?" the man asked.

"Yes. We were on a call, and they stopped to ask for some information."

Then I heard their siren start and wheels screech as they took off. I ran to the front door. There stood Oscar by the van. But the cops were nowhere in sight.

As I came bounding down the steps, Oscar ran toward me. "I can't believe it!" he said. "I just can't believe it! I was standing there with a cop on either side of me and thinking about Attica. I mean, I knew it was all over for me. The next thing I knew those two clowns heard something on their radio. One of them went over and then screamed to his buddy, 'Get in! We may have a police killing three blocks over!' "

I smiled knowingly as Oscar continued, "I mean, those dudes took off as though they were shot out of a cannon!"

When I laughed, Oscar said, "Hey, wait a minute! Lefty, did you have something to do with this?"

"Oldest trick in the book, Oscar," I said. "I just called the emergency number and told them a cop got shot three blocks from here and that I noticed this squad car right out front. I mean, every cop within twenty blocks will converge on that corner. You know as well as I that if a cop gets shot, the whole force will rise up to defend him."

"You rascal," Oscar said admiringly. "I have to admit

you pulled a good one that time. But so help me, when I saw you bounding up those steps leaving me with those two cops, I knew you were number one on my hit list. Man, you don't know how close I came to pulling my gun—not on those cops, but on you! I couldn't imagine my old buddy leaving me to face the music all alone."

"Oh, come on, Oscar. You know better than that. I mean, if they busted you, you'd have to kick the habit cold turkey in jail. I wouldn't want that to happen to you."

I jumped into the van and said, "Okay, let's go to Seventy-sixth Street while all the cops are busy on Eighty-second. This should be quick."

The address I had picked out of the phone book was a beautiful apartment house.

"Let me handle this," I told Oscar. "Remember, we're just TV repairmen going to Thelma Avedon's apartment. I'm Arnie, you're Morris."

"Yes," Oscar said, grinning. "I'm Morris, the cat burglar!"

As we headed toward the door, I spotted a security guard. How were we going to get by him?

"Thelma Avedon called and asked us to take a look at her TV set," I told him when he asked what we wanted.

The guard rubbed his chin. "That's strange," he said. "She didn't mention anything to me about that when she left earlier this morning."

I knew I'd better bluff. At least I'd found out she wasn't home.

"Isn't that just like her!" I exclaimed. "She is as forgetful as can be. I remember when we sold her a TV set. She called us and read us the riot act because it wouldn't work. I asked her whether she had plugged it in. She said she'd forgotten that!"

The guard laughed. "Yes, she's getting kind of old and

forgetful. And just between us, has she got a temper!"

"I know!" I replied. "She was really giving me a going over about that TV set. She accused our company of being a bunch of crooks trying to take advantage of an old lady. She threatened to call the mayor. She even threatened to come down and shoot the salesman!"

"Really?" the guard asked eagerly—anxious for the juicy gossip about one of the apartment dwellers. "I didn't think she was quite that bad."

"Bad? Let me tell you something else, sir." I edged closer and said confidentially, "She said if we didn't get her TV working within the hour, she was coming down to our store and blowing it up! Can you imagine!"

"You never know about these little old ladies," the guard said, laughing. "Sometimes they could carry sticks of dynamite in their big purses!"

He was still laughing as he opened the door for us to enter.

"Oops," I said. "Forgot to ask which was her apartment. I left my work sheet out in the van."

"It's seven hundred thirty-nine."

"Thanks. I remember now."

When we were safely in the elevator, Oscar said, "Come on, Lefty, you don't know this Thelma Avedon, do you?"

"No, I just got her name out of the book. I just had to bluff back there with the guard. Fortunately, it came out okay. And from what he said, it sounds as if the lady hasn't come back yet. So we're in luck. If she doesn't answer the doorbell, I have a special key that will let us in. If she answers the door, well, I'll just come up with another excuse."

When we got to 739, I pushed the buzzer. No one answered. I pushed again and again. No answer.

I pulled out a slim plastic card, pushed it against the door lock, and wiggled it a few times. The door opened readily.

We quickly stepped inside and shut the door behind us. "We have to be quick," I whispered.

We dashed into the living room. There, along one wall, was a big console TV—just the kind that Abe would like. I pulled it out from the wall, unplugged it, and said, "Oscar, help me get the back off it."

"What for?"

"Because we're going to go through this place looking for small valuables—jewels, silver, you know. We'll stash them inside here, and then we'll carry this TV down to the 'shop' for repairs."

"Gotcha!" Oscar replied. "Good thinking, Lefty!"

He went into the bedroom, and I started through the dining room. We made trip after trip to the TV set, our hands loaded with expensive jewelry and accessories, squeezing them into every available nook and cranny inside that set. I even searched through the heat registers and in one found a box containing cold cash. I put the money in my pocket and threw the box down. No sense in taking up room with it.

"We'd better get out of here," Oscar said nervously. "That old lady could be back any minute."

"Right! Let's slap this back on the set and get out of here."

When we picked up the set to move it into the hall, we discovered it was really heavy. Oscar groaned.

"I know you're getting sick," I said, "but just think how sick you're going to be if they catch you and throw you in the slammer. Then it'll be cold turkey!"

That gave Oscar a burst of energy.

We moved the set into the hall and carefully locked the apartment door behind us. Then we headed for the elevator.

It seemed like an eternity waiting for that elevator because a guy came out into the hall and started our way. "Hey, wait a minute," he called. "I want to talk to you." Oh, no! He was trying to stall us. Maybe somebody had already called the cops. Or maybe he heard us in Thelma Avedon's apartment!

"Gently put this thing onto the floor—in case we have to go for our guns," I whispered to Oscar.

"Lefty, don't go for your gun unless you absolutely have to," Oscar whispered back. "If that guard at the door hears a gunshot, there'll be no way we can get out of this place!"

"I'll take hostages before I let them take me," I snarled.

By this time the man was almost up to us. "What are you two doing here?" he demanded.

"We're from Pennyington's TV Sales and Service," I said. "Thelma Avedon's TV set needed to be repaired. Why?"

"That's what I thought," he said. "Would you believe my set just went on the blink, and I wanted to watch the game tonight. Would you take a look at it while you're here?"

My heart had been going ninety miles an hour, but it slowed a little when I heard what the man said. But we still had to get rid of him.

"Do you know Thelma Avedon?" I asked.

"Sure do. She's been living here twenty years, just as we have."

"Then you probably know what she's like," I went on. "If we don't get this set repaired right away, she claims she's going to blow up our company. We thought we could fix the set in her apartment, but we don't have all the equipment with us that we need. So we're going to have to take it to the shop. As soon as we do that, I'll come back and check on yours. It shouldn't take too long. Yours probably just needs a new tube. It'll be working before that game."

"Thanks," he said. "You're sure right about Thelma. She's got quite a temper."

The elevator door had opened, and Oscar was holding it open. We both lifted the set and scooted it into the elevator. As the door shut, we waved to the man.

"Wow, that was close!" I said.

"Lefty, you have the mind of a genius!" Oscar said. "You keep thinking ahead. Now let's hope we make it all the way past that guard."

As we got off the elevator on the first floor, I looked toward the entrance. The guard saw us coming. If he went for his gun, there'd be no way we could drop the TV set and go for ours.

"Problems?" he asked.

"Yes. We couldn't figure it out. I've got some special tools down at the shop. I just hope we can get this thing fixed and back here before Thelma gets back. You know how she is!"

The guard obligingly opened the door for us, and Oscar and I really moved to get that set into the van.

In moments we had the set inside the van and we took off, tires squealing. I'll bet that guard thought we were the most dedicated TV repairmen he had ever seen! I also wondered about something else. How much money were we going to get for all of that loot?

Our next stop would be at Abe Steinman's. He had just the right shop for a TV set like this one!

When we pulled up in front, I said to Oscar, "You stay here and watch this stuff. I'll be right back."

But as I bounded up the steps to Abe's place, a thought hit me: *As soon as I get inside that door, Oscar's going to grab those keys and drive off.* He was a junkie. I was a junkie. And I knew better than to ever trust any junkie—especially one who was getting sick and needed a quick shot.

So I wheeled around, ran back to the van, and pulled the keys out of the ignition. "Hey, man, what are you doing that for?" Oscar demanded.

I didn't want to make Oscar mad, so I could hardly tell him the truth. "Oscar, when I walk in there, I want to surprise Abe. Not only do I have a TV set with a lot of goodies in it but I also want to see his eyes when I hand him the keys to the van. We should get a pretty good price for this van, don't you think?"

"Yeah, man, we sure should!" Oscar exclaimed excitedly.

Going back up the steps, I waited a minute. Then I pushed the buzzer. When Abe answered, I said, "Abe, my good brother, I have some goodies for you."

"Another TV set?" he asked, rubbing his hands together in delight.

"Man, I've got it all: TV set, jewelry, silverware. You want it?"

"Sure do. Bring it in."

Oscar groaned again as we carried the TV set in. I told him I had no idea what we should ask for it.

"I think Abe'll go over each item in detail," he said, "and I think he'll give us fair market price."

Abe didn't say much when we carried the set in. But when we pulled the back off and started pulling out silver and jewelry, his eyes bugged out.

"Pretty clever! Pretty clever!" he said.

He took us back into his office and began to tally up all the stuff. Then I held up the keys to the van. "You want to sell it, too?" he asked.

"Yes, let's figure it all up."

"Okay," he said, "the TV set is two hundred dollars. And

I'll give you three thousand dollars for the jewelry and silver. And two thousand dollars for the van. That's a total of five thousand, two hundred dollars."

Two thousand for the van sounded a little low to me. "Come on, Abe. You can do better than that on the van."

"What are you talking about, Lefty? Don't you know I have to sell this stuff? And the reason people buy from me is that they think they're getting a real bargain. So I have to price it at what the market will bear. And let me tell you, kid, it gets really risky in this business. One false move, and the cops will be in here to shut me down and send me away. I really won't get much more than two thousand dollars for that van. So if you don't like what I'm offering, just take your keys back and drive it away. I'm giving you the best price in the neighborhood."

"I think he's right, Lefty," Oscar chimed in. "Let's just take our money and split."

I didn't know whether or not to trust Oscar's judgment. He had his mind on one thing—getting high.

"Well, okay," I finally said. "But it sure seems as though we should have gotten a lot more for that van."

"Tell you what," Abe said. "Why don't you guys have a drink on me? Maybe that will square it."

He motioned toward his wet bar, telling us to help ourselves while he put some of the jewelry away. But before he did, he counted out five thousand, two hundred dollars and gave it to me. Right away, I gave Oscar his half.

We were sitting there, finishing our drinks, when Abe came back. "Notice my pictures?" he asked.

"Notice them? How could anybody not notice them?" I responded.

"You want to buy one?" Abe asked.

I sure wouldn't have minded having one. But my mind was on one thing—the same thing Oscar's was on. That money was burning a hole in my pocket. Now I could really get my mountain of heroin.

Abe persisted about the pictures, pulling me over to look more closely at them. "This one's my sister," he announced.

"Abe, you're kidding," I answered. "You let your sister do things like that? I sure wouldn't let my sister do something like that!"

Abe laughed. "No, she's not my sister. There was a big hole in the plaster, and I thought that picture looked a lot better than a hole in the wall."

Oscar was getting anxious to leave, so we finished our drinks. We shook hands with Abe, and he said, "Come back again, boys. I'll always be here."

How could he be so sure?

12

We had gotten only about a half a block from Abe's when we heard him shouting after us: "Lefty! Oscar! Wait!"

He ran up to us, breathless. "I just heard a news broadcast," he said. "Something about two TV repairmen killing a cop up on East Eighty-second Street."

"What?" I yelled. "Two TV repairmen killing a cop on Eighty-second. But—"

"Lefty, for crying out loud," Oscar interrupted. "That's from that telephone call you made so we could get away from those cops."

"I didn't get the details," Abe went on. "All I could think of was you two guys walking down the street with those TV repairmen's coveralls on. So help me, if you guys knocked off a cop, you're in real trouble."

"Not so fast, Abe. We're not into cop killing."

He looked at me in disbelief. I guess he knew I'd kill a cop if one of them got in my way. Then he said, "Don't walk down the street wearing those coveralls. Everybody in New York City will be looking for TV repairmen! You guys are going to get nailed for sure if you don't get those things off!"

Abe might be wrong about a cop getting killed, but he was right about what everybody would be looking for. I unzipped mine and slipped out of them so fast it probably set a world's record. Oscar was out of his with lightning speed, too. We wadded them up, and I headed for the nearest garbage can. When I opened the lid, I noticed maggots eating the stinking garbage inside. The stench was enough to turn anyone's stomach. I held my breath, stuffed the coveralls down inside, and slammed the lid back on.

"Well, that's that," I said matter-of-factly. "We just stuffed two TV repairmen into the garbage. The maggots are already eating them. The way they'll soon be eating that cop who got it!"

Abe blanched. "Listen, you guys, there's one thing you'd better get straight," he said. "No matter what happens, don't ever drop a cop. I mean, don't *ever* shoot a cop!"

Strange advice coming from a fence.

"Hey, Abe, what's bugging you, man?"

He hesitated. Then he stammered, "My brother's a cop."

So that was it. Abe must have worried that if we dropped a cop, it might be his brother.

"Abe," I said, "everybody's got problems. So you have a brother who's a cop. Big deal. But you have our word. We won't ever drop a cop."

Oscar didn't say anything. I was pretty sure he wouldn't

agree with me. But I knew he was in no mood to argue right now.

"I really think a lot of my brother," Abe went on, "even though he is a cop. You see, one winter he and I were walking on some ice, and I broke through into that icy water. I panicked, trying to catch my breath. Next thing I knew, someone grabbed me and hauled me up. I hit the surface of that water gasping for breath. He pulled me to safety. My brother saved my life!"

"Okay, Abe, no dropping cops," I repeated. "I can see your brother's pretty special to you."

"Man, let's get out of here," Oscar urged.

"Abe, we have to go. You understand."

He nodded and turned to go back to his place. We headed on toward the home neighborhood.

I was still thinking about Abe and his brother. Had his brother really saved his life—or was he just trying to get us to avoid a shoot-out? Did he even have a brother?

Still wondering, I turned around to glimpse the big guy again. But what I saw made me gasp. Abe apparently hadn't gone back to his place. He had waited for us to get down the street a little way, and he had gone back to that garbage can. He had his fingers over his nose as he lifted the lid, pulled those TV repairmen's coveralls out, and shook the filthy garbage and maggots off them.

"Abe," I called, "what are you doing?"

He looked up but didn't answer. He just took off running toward his place.

"Oscar, did you see that?" I asked.

"Yes," Oscar responded, "those fences are all alike. He can't stand to see anything going to waste. Now that he's got that van, he'll probably sell those coveralls to some young kid and tell him how he can make a mint."

"But doesn't he realize the cops are looking for two TV repairmen? I mean, he just told us that."

"Lefty, those fences have no hearts," Oscar replied. "He won't worry about what happens to the guy who buys them. Besides, he's not going to sell them today. He's planning for the future."

I wished I could believe what Oscar was saying, but somehow the whole thing just didn't add up. Later I would discover how the pieces of the puzzle fit together. But right now it really didn't seem important enough to worry about. For Oscar and for me the most important thing was to find Spino.

He was in the same spot. And was he surprised when we told him we wanted to buy five thousand dollars' worth of dope. Obviously he didn't have that much with him. But he told us to wait and he'd be right back. He insisted on seeing our money, and we showed him that. But we weren't about to pay him till he brought us the dope.

"Hurry!" Oscar called after him. "I can't wait much longer!"

We probably could have copped from somebody else. But I sure didn't want to upset Spino—not after that run-in with O'Reilly. And Spino did have good stuff.

Oscar and I leaned up against a wall, waiting. A man walked up and stopped in front of us. He looked like a cop, a decoy, and my heart began to beat faster. Here I was with several thousand dollars on me. What a time to get busted! I slowly dropped my left hand toward my belt. But then something hit me. What if this were Abe's brother? If I dropped him, I could forget ever taking anything to Abe again!

The guy stationed himself in front of me and looked me straight in the eye. He surely wasn't a junkie, and he didn't seem to be afraid. He had to be a cop. I kept searching for his backup.

"Hi," he said pleasantly. "I'm Reverend Benton from the Walter Hoving Home upstate in Garrison. Here's something for you to read."

He stood there holding out a little piece of paper. I figured it was a ploy. As soon as I reached for it, he'd whip out his gun. No sir! I wasn't going to be suckered into taking my hand away from my gun. Did he think I was stupid?

He said it again: "Here's something for you to read."

"Sorry, man, I can't read. I'm a dropout."

He laughed—a deep, infectious laugh. "I tell you what," he said, "just stick this in your pocket. Maybe someday you'll need it."

"What kind of a paper is it?" I asked suspiciously.

"It's called a tract," he said. "The title is *A Positive Cure for Drug Addiction*. And, you know, there *is* a cure."

"Man, I'm no junkie," I said in disgust. "You take me for a junkie? I mean, they ought to run all those junkies out of town. I don't need a cure."

I talked big, but I could tell I hadn't convinced this guy.

"Have it your way," he said, "but why don't you take this and pass it on to someone else—maybe one of your friends who is on drugs and could use help."

With that, the reverend pushed the tract toward my pocket. I moved my hand a couple of inches, grabbed the paper, and shoved it into my pocket.

"Sure, I'll give it to someone who needs it," I said. "Thanks. Thanks a lot."

Oscar hadn't said anything the whole time. I guess he was trying to figure this guy out, too.

I thought the guy would leave when I took his paper, but he didn't. "Listen, let me level with you guys," he said. "I know you are both on it and need help. And let me tell you something else. I'm no cop."

He smiled and pulled back his jacket to show us he wasn't armed. Somehow I couldn't help but like the guy. But I sure couldn't figure out what he was up to.

"Let's go through this once more," I said. "You're who from where?"

"Reverend Benton from the Walter Hoving Home. My wife and I have a home in upstate New York for girls who have been addicts, alcoholics, and delinquents. They come to us for help."

"Do I look like a girl?" I sneered.

He chuckled. "Of course not. Now maybe some of our girls would be delighted if you came up and joined our program. We can't do that, but we do have a boys' program located in Brooklyn. It's called Teen Challenge."

"Teen Challenge?" I questioned. "Must be something for teenagers."

"No, it isn't just for teenagers. We take in older people, too. We've had some old-time junkies who hobbled in from the street. I guess they must have been around fifty. Most junkies, you know, don't live that long. But they weren't dead yet, and we were able to help them. Today they are completely clean."

"Are you kidding?" Oscar said. "I've never seen a clean junkie in my whole life."

"There are plenty of them now because of the Teen Challenge program," the reverend went on. "Christ changed their lives."

"Christ changed their lives?" I asked. "I've never heard of that, but. . . ."

My words trailed off in midair because just then a blue and white police car pulled up at the curb right beside us. Two cops jumped out and headed our way.

This Benton guy must be a decoy cop. He was just stalling us until his partners got here. Yes, that was it! Oscar had told me before that sometimes these decoys posed as ministers.

"Okay, bust it up. Get moving," one cop called as they approached.

Oscar and I started to obey, but Reverend Benton stood his ground. "Wait a minute, officer," he said, politely but firmly. "I was talking to these two gentlemen about—"

"I don't care if you were talking to your mother," the cop returned. "I said, move it!"

The reverend stiffened. "Hey, officer, I don't want to appear nasty or anything, but is this America?"

"Don't get smart, buddy," the cop said. "Move it!"

Reverend Benton reached for his pocket. I knew he didn't have a gun, but the cop didn't know that—and he went for his. But the reverend just pulled out his wallet and showed some identification.

"I'm Reverend Benton from the Walter Hoving Home," he said. "I am a minister of the Gospel, and I was sharing that Good News with these two gentlemen. I believe the Constitution guarantees me—"

"Preacher, don't start quoting the Constitution to me," the cop said. "It's been a rough day. I have orders from my sergeant to move everybody. And that includes you. Now move it!"

Reverend Benton was really getting agitated. "Officer, do I need to remind you that this is America?" he said. "We have some rights in this country, and one of those rights is to be able to assemble peaceably. I've got some good things I want to tell these two gentlemen, and I don't think you can stop me."

The officer started to walk away and motioned for Reverend Benton to follow. I walked a few feet in the other direction and stopped to watch. They were too far away for me to hear all they said, but the preacher was waving his arms around. The officer just stood there with his arms folded across his chest. It seemed as though the preacher was doing all the talking.

Suddenly the two officers walked back to their car, and Reverend Benton walked back to us. I was a little more ready to listen to what he had to say now. I liked him. Nobody pushed him around. Besides, he had gotten those cops to leave—and I liked anybody who got the cops out of the way!

"Reverend," I said, "didn't you know you could get busted for not obeying the order of an officer?"

He laughed. "Oh, that would be okay. They'd just put me in jail and I'd have a wonderful opportunity to tell all the other prisoners about how Christ could set them free."

What a guy! He could even see good in going to jail!

"What did you tell that cop?" Oscar asked.

"Well, he told me he was just trying to do his duty. He said his sergeant didn't want crowds to congregate on the streets because of the junkies. I told him to get his sergeant, and I'd talk to him. Probably the sergeant will come back and bust me. But, as I say, I'll tell people about Christ no matter where I am."

I laughed. "Hey, I can see the headlines now. 'Preacher Gets Busted for Telling Junkies About Religion.'"

"Hey," he said, "that's sort of how David Wilkerson, the founder of Teen Challenge, got started in this work. Years ago he came to this city to try to talk to some gang members who were charged with crimes. He stood up in court to say something. The judge, whose life had been threatened, misinterpreted David's motives and ordered him thrown out of court. The next day the papers carried a picture of the Bible-waving preacher being thrown out of court. Well, that gave him an inside track with the gang members. And God helped him launch a ministry to drug addicts and delinquents. Now it goes all around the world!"

While he was telling us this story, another guy walked up. "Hey, Brother Benton," he said, "what was going on back here? What did those cops want?"

"Oh, Victor, they're nervous about people congregating on the sidewalks. I might get busted in a few minutes. Stick around and take pictures. You can send them to my wife— and maybe to the newspapers, too."

He laughed that infectious laugh again, and Oscar and I joined in. Then, turning toward me, the reverend said, "This is Victor Hernandez. He's a graduate of our Teen Challenge program."

I looked Victor over. He had all the signs of being a junkie. But was he really clean?

"Victor, why don't you tell these two gentlemen what happened to you?" Reverend Benton suggested.

Victor started to say something, and then he stopped and stared at Oscar. "Hey," he exclaimed, "you're Oscar Rodriguez, aren't you?"

Oscar's eyes widened. "Yes. But how did you know me?"

"Oscar, you don't remember me, do you?" Victor said. "Five years ago I used to walk these streets with you. One time we broke into an apartment together. Remember?"

"Oh, wow!" Oscar said, "sure I remember. But Victor, you've really changed. What's happened?"

Grinning from ear to ear, Victor said, "Oscar, Christ not only changed me on the inside but He also changed the outside."

"I can't believe it!" Oscar said.

"Well, I remember when you got sent up," Victor went on. "I was at the bottom. I mean, you know as well as I do what I had to do to get the money to support my habit. And about four years ago I almost ended up dead of an over-dose.

"I was so sick one morning," he went on, "that I couldn't get out of bed to find the usual place where I took my morning fix . . . and my afternoon fix . . . and my evening fix. I guess you guys know all about that."

We nodded.

"So I yelled to my brother, Chuck. When he came, I told him I was too sick to go out, so would he get my works for me."

My mind went to my brother, Nicky. I wondered what he was doing. Was he on junk yet? Had he started because I started?

"Chuck brought me my works," Victor went on, "and I told him to get me a glass of water. The pain in my body was growing worse. My fix had been at about seven the previous evening. By now the muscles in my arms and legs tightened. My whole body was tense, and the first stages of stomach cramps were coming on. My nose was running and my head was aching."

By that description I knew that Victor had been there.

" 'I got a bag of stuff from the cabinet,' Chuck told me. Like a good boy he had gathered up all my instruments of death. I got it going, and in a few seconds the snow white powder was oozing through my veins. But just as I was ex-pecting to enjoy the high, I rolled off the side of the bed and onto the floor. The drug was too strong. I had overdosed! The power of that heroin rushed to my heart so fast that it knocked me unconscious. In fact, it happened so quickly that I didn't even have time to pull out the needle. When Chuck found me ten minutes later, my whole arm was bloody."

I could hardly believe that description. It was almost ex-actly what had happened to me!

"Chuck yelled for my mom, and together they got me back into bed. I came around enough to pull the needle out of my arm. Mom, bless her heart, was sobbing, but she said she was relieved to know her son was still alive, even if he was a dope fiend. She hugged me to her bosom and cried, "Victor, Victor, don't you see what you are doing to yourself and to me and to Chuckie? You're killing us all, son."

He wiped a tear from his eye before he continued. I could tell it was hurting him to call back those painful memories.

"As Mom went out the door, she broke down and started to sob so pitifully, I knew what she was thinking. If I didn't change my way of life, I'd soon be dead. Mom came back to the side of the bed, sat down, and asked me if I'd consider going into the Teen Challenge program in Brooklyn. Well, to tell you the truth, I'd about had it with programs. I'd been detoxified so many times I couldn't even remember them all. I'd seen psychiatrists. I'd been in and out of hospitals. I'd done time in jail. Nothing helped. So the last thing I wanted was another program. But Mom insisted this one would help me.

"So I went to Brooklyn. As soon as I walked in that door, I was greeted by former addicts. In fact, Oscar, do you remember Carlos? He used to get off with us sometimes. Well, he was the first guy I ran into at Teen Challenge. And did he look clean! I mean, completely changed.

"Well, to please my mom I went into their program. I began to kick the habit. I mean, kick it cold. But God did a beautiful thing. I was healed of kicking. I mean, I couldn't believe it. I had no problems whatsoever! It was almost scary! Then another beautiful thing happened. I figured if Jesus could do that much for me, the only logical thing was for me to give my heart to Him and ask Him to be my Saviour and Lord. Well, He came in, and I got rid of all those old filthy habits I used to have. He took out the desire for drugs and placed within me a desire to help other people. I've been clean for about four years now. Christ did that for me. And He can do it for you, too."

This whole thing was just too fantastic for me to believe it was real.

"You know," Reverend Benton said, "it's not just by chance that the four of us met here today. I believe God sent Victor and me to find you two. Why don't you guys give your lives over to Jesus and join us at Teen Challenge? I believe He really wants to do something great for both of you."

I still wasn't sure that this could be for real. Then out of the corner of my eye, I saw Spino. He was leaning up against the wall, watching us. And he was smiling—so he had the stuff.

Oscar spotted him, too—and Oscar was anxious to cop. And we sure didn't want to wait around until that police sergeant came back.

"Victor," I said, knowing he would understand, "we have business right now. Okay?"

"Okay," he said. "And it's been great talking to you. Let me give you a tract."

"The reverend already did," I said. "But I think Oscar would like one."

Victor handed one to Oscar, then he and the reverend turned and walked down the street.

When they were gone, we headed over to Spino. He was holding a package in his hands, and before long he had our money and we had the package. I didn't know it then, but this would be the last time I'd ever buy dope. Events were closing in on me—events which were going to alter the course of my life.

13

Oscar and I laid up for a couple of weeks, getting high several times every day. In fact, I don't think we ever came down. We still had some dope left, but we were getting on each other's nerves, cooped up in that filthy apartment, so we started to hit the streets again.

One evening when he was feeling especially daring, Oscar said, "Why don't we go over and rob Abe Steinman?"

"What?" I yelled. "I never heard of anybody robbing a fence. What would we do with the stuff we stole from him?"

"Stupid!" Oscar gruffly replied. "Not the stuff. The money from that cash box. Don't you remember how much money he keeps in that box? He pulled out over five thousand dollars to pay you the last time, and he still had plenty left in it. I'll bet he's got money stashed all over the place. If we went over there and stuck a gun to his head, he'd start squealing like a pig. Fences usually have a yellow streak in them, anyway."

"Yes, but won't he have bodyguards around?"

"I've never seen any."

"Well, I saw a couple of big guys around there once," I said.

"Probably some of Abe's relatives, learning the business," Oscar countered. "Besides, we can surprise them and rob them, too!"

"Sounds as though you're feeling pretty brave, Oscar."

"Sounds as though you're getting a little chicken, Lefty. What's happened to that brave man who was gung ho to show me how to make money? Have you lost your nerve?"

Oscar knew I couldn't stand anybody inferring I was a coward, so we headed over toward Abe's place.

It didn't take us long to get there. As we reached the door, I pulled out my revolver. Five bullets. That should be enough. Oscar checked his, too. "I'm loaded," he told me.

We knocked. No answer.

"That's funny," Oscar said. "I thought he was always here."

We knocked some more. Still no answer.

"Maybe he's gone out for dinner," I said. "It's kind of late for that, but he must get hungry here. He'll probably be right back."

"If he's gone, then I think our luck favors us," Oscar said. "I've got a great idea."

"What's that?"

"This is going to be so simple I just can't believe it!" Oscar said. "All we do is walk in and take whatever we want. We won't even need to use our guns!"

That suited me just fine. I'd much rather steal than have to take a chance with a gun.

I banged on the door louder—to make sure no one was there. Then I kicked the door. Nothing. I pulled out my plastic card and pushed it against the lock. Nothing happened. I squinted to see what was the matter. Oh, no! It was double-locked with two bolts. No way was any plastic card going to open that door. I should have known Abe would protect his place against burglars.

"Stand back!" Oscar ordered. He aimed his gun at the lock and squeezed the trigger. The explosion was deafening, and wood and metal sprayed everywhere. And when

Oscar grabbed the door handle and jerked, the door came flying open.

With guns drawn, we edged inside. And were we in for a surprise! There was nothing in that room. It was absolutely empty!

"What do you make of this?" Oscar asked.

"I don't know. Let's check the office."

It, too, was locked. This time it was my gun that split the lock open. And when we moved inside, we got the same kind of shock. It was completely cleared out. The only evidence that Abe had been here was the plush carpet on the floor.

"Do you suppose Abe got busted?" Oscar asked.

I didn't answer. Instead, I looked around some more. Finally I said, "Oscar, let's get out of here, quickly. I smell a rat. We may be in a trap!"

"Oh, come on, Lefty. You're too nervous about things. I'll bet a thousand to one Abe got busted. No problem."

"No problem? No problem? You think that's no problem, Oscar? Well, if Abe got busted, that means they've got him down at the police station, and they are grilling him good. He's probably going to start singing, Oscar. He's going to name names. You know whose names he's going to name, Oscar? Yours and mine! Oscar, this whole thing is wrong. We have to get out of here!"

He headed toward the front door—the way we came in. "No way, Oscar," I whispered. "You head out that door, and they may gun you down. This whole thing is wrong!"

I headed for some inside steps that went to the roof of the tenement. I could check things out from up there. Oscar decided to follow, and we quickly ran up to the top.

Once out on the rooftop, I cautiously made my way to the edge, got on my stomach, and peered over the side. I looked up the street. Nothing unusual. I looked down the street. Nothing unusual. Then I looked across the street. What I saw made my hair stand on end.

"Come here, Oscar," I whispered. "Take a look at this. Then tell me whether you still feel I'm being too nervous."

He crawled up next to me. I pointed across the street. "Look over there. No, on the second story. Look at that window. Tell me what you see."

Oscar squinted. "Oh, wow! We almost got it, didn't we?"

What we both saw were two men peering out that window—with rifles aimed over at Abe's door. Cops! And they were waiting for us to come out!

Down the street I spotted a van. When I called it to Oscar's attention, he said, "Man, I'll bet that van is loaded with cops. We have to get out of here. Now!"

We edged away from where we could be seen and, bending over as far as we could, we kept running across tenement rooftops clear to the other side of the block. Then we went down the stairs of that last one and hit the street again.

We then hurried back to our own neighborhood, still rather shaken from our experience. When we noticed two junkies at the corner, we went up to them. "Hey, Julio; hey, Frankie," I called. "You guys know about Abe Steinman's place? It's empty. That fence is gone."

"Haven't you heard?" Julio asked.

"Heard what?" Oscar and I said in unison.

"Last night two guys went over there to rob Abe," Julio said. "I mean, there was this big shoot-out. Those two guys got killed. But you're never going to believe this part."

"Go on! Go on!" I said eagerly.

"They shot Abe in the leg. And when they did, cops came out from everywhere to defend Abe."

"Didn't they know Abe was a fence?" I said, laughing.

"It's not funny, Lefty," Julio told me. "You may not believe this, but that whole operation was nothing but a front. Abe's an undercover cop! The cops set up that whole fencing operation to get at the junkies in the area!"

"Oh, I can't believe that," I said. "We knew Abe. His brother is a cop; but he was really embarrassed by that. Oscar and I sold Abe a bunch of stuff. He gave us a fair price."

Frankie let out a low whistle. "Oh, wow! That means you guys are on the cops' hit list."

The whole idea really unnerved me, but then I thought of something. "Oh, they don't have anything on us. It would be Abe's word against ours."

"That's what you think!" Julio interjected. "I'll bet they've got the evidence against you."

"Well, Abe's been out on the street looking for you two," Frankie said. "He must think he's got some evidence."

"Lefty, did Abe ever offer you a drink?" Julio asked.

"Yes. Why?"

"Don't you know that when you poured that drink, you left your fingerprints all over that bottle?"

I blanched.

"That isn't all," Julio continued. "Did you spend time looking at the pictures of those nudes in his office?"

"Yes, but that's not against the law."

"You dummies," Julio said. "There was a hidden TV camera behind them. All the while you were looking at those pictures, you were staring right into the lens of a TV camera. Man, they have you on tape. They have the evidence!"

"Lefty, we've been set up!" Oscar yelled. "It's all over!"

Julio saw our consternation and added some more fuel to

the fire. "Something else," he said. "When Abe was seen around, he had a couple of pairs of TV repairmen's coveralls with him."

My mouth flew open. Now it all fit together. That's why Abe pulled those out of that filthy garbage can. He wanted them for evidence!

I whirled around and began studying the street. Abe and his cop friends could be anywhere. They could show up at any minute. And Abe knew where we lived.

"We can't go back to the apartment," Oscar said. "They probably have the place staked out."

But where could we go? "Hey, maybe I could go home to my mother's," I said. "Maybe she'll take me in. I can turn on the tears and tell her how sorry I am—"

"Okay," Oscar interrupted. "It's you and me against the world, little buddy. Here's hoping we don't end up in Attica."

The word *Attica* terrified me. I'd heard it was one of the worst prisons in America. If you didn't submit to the system, someone would ram a knife through you. No way did I want to go to Attica.

We separated, but before I had gone a few steps, Oscar ran back to me. "I know we're hot," he whispered. "Any minute now we could get busted. But whatever you do, don't get caught with your revolver on you. If they can't nail you for something else, they'll nail you for possession of a dangerous weapon. And make sure you don't have any works or stuff on you. When they bust you, be sure you're clean. They'll go easier on you."

"What'll I do with this gun?"

"Let's walk up this alley and stash it."

About halfway up the alley were a bunch of beat-up garbage cans. Behind them was a big crack in the wall. We stashed our guns there and pushed some garbage over them. Then we walked out of the alley, and I headed home. Would I ever see Oscar again?

It didn't take long to walk the few blocks to where my mother lived. And, surprisingly, when she opened the door and saw me, she threw her arms around me and hugged me. "Oh, I'm so glad to see you, Lefty," she said. And it sounded as though she really meant it. Then she added, "Just this morning the police were here looking for you. I thought for sure you were dead."

"The police?" I asked, trying not to let the panic show. "What did they want? What did you tell them?"

"I told them the truth, Lefty. I said I hadn't seen you since you left home a few months ago."

Was that all it had been—a few months? It felt like years!

"Mom, is it okay if I stay here for a few days?"

"Of course, honey. Those cops said they would drop by here later. I'm sure you can explain the whole situation to them."

I shoved her aside, yelling, "I don't want any cops talking to me; do you understand? I have to get out of here!"

As I ran down the hall, I could hear her calling, "Lefty! Lefty! Don't run! Don't run! That's not the answer!"

Her words echoed in my mind as I just kept on running. After all, running was the only answer I knew.

Down the hall, down the stairs, out into the street I ran. And as I ran along the sidewalk, I glanced back and noticed a dark-colored car pull out from the curb and slowly follow me. Oh, no! Rats! Those cops must have staked out my mother's place, expecting me to show up there.

I ran faster, but my legs were no match for a car. Only one thing to do—go where a car couldn't go. So I leaped a nearby fence and tore through a backyard. I heard brakes screech and car doors slam. I knew they were on my tail. Instinctively I reached for my gun. Stupid me! I forgot I had stashed it.

I spotted a little darkened doorway. It would lead to the other street. I hoped those cops weren't close enough to see me go through it.

But when I got to the street, I saw two policemen just ahead, so I darted into a tenement and took off for the roof. This way of escape had never failed me yet.

Sheer panic was taking its toll as I struggled up those steps. My strength almost exhausted, at last I burst onto the rooftop and started running across.

"Stop, or I'll shoot!" a gruff voice behind me said.

I wasn't about to stop. I just kept running.

"Stop, or I'll shoot!" the voice commanded, louder, more insistent this time. I kept running.

And then I heard the shot. But I felt nothing, so I kept moving. Another command to stop. And when I didn't, I heard another shot. Then I felt it. A piercing pain shot through my leg, and I went tumbling across the rooftop.

Rolling over and screaming and cursing and grabbing for my leg, I felt a huge hand grab me and slap on handcuffs. Then cops came running from other rooftops and converged on me, surrounding me. I didn't care. All I was really aware of was excruciating pain.

One of those officers took a look at the blood oozing out of my leg. He took his handkerchief and applied some pressure and then tied the handkerchief around it. He said something about its not being too bad. Too bad? The pain was killing me.

A couple of other officers roughly hauled me to my feet and started searching me. They even turned my pockets inside out. I think they were surprised that they didn't find one thing.

They all surrounded me as they helped me down the stairs, out onto the street, and into a waiting patrol car. I had come to the end of the road.

Down at the police station they read me my rights; then they booked me. Another officer looked at my leg and said they'd better take me to the emergency room at the hospital. Through my pain a plan started forming in my mind. When I got to the hospital, away from these cops, I'd start running again.

But the cops must have figured I'd try something like that. They kept three cops with me constantly in the hospital.

A doctor gave me a local anesthetic, cleaned the wound, and bandaged it. He said I was going to be all right. I wasn't so sure. All I could think of was Attica Prison.

Back at the station they took me once again into that little room, still handcuffed. Then the door opened, and in walked Abe.

"Lefty," he said, "you were one of my best customers. I sure hate to see you here."

How was I supposed to respond to that?

"I don't know whether you're planning to give us a bad time, Lefty," he continued, "but we really have the goods on you. We have your fingerprints on all sorts of things. We have you on videotape. We have the coveralls. You don't have a chance."

So what Julio had told us was really true!

"I'll bet we got a hundred guys on this bust," Abe went on. "And you were one of the big ones!"

"How about Oscar?" I asked.

"We haven't nabbed him yet. But we'll get him. We have fifty men combing that neighborhood. This may take care of a few junkies for a long time."

And I couldn't keep from wondering: *How long?*

The next day I was taken to 100 Center Street to appear before a judge. At the arraignment I pleaded guilty. I knew there was no sense in fighting. The evidence was too great.

Then they took me back to jail for a few more days before my sentencing—something about the court conducting an investigation.

Five days later I stood before the judge for sentencing. I knew Attica Prison was going to be my address for a good, long time. What I didn't know was that that judge's decision was going to change my life dramatically!

14

I tried not to look it, but I was terrified as I stood before the sentencing judge and he stared down at me. "Your name is Lefty Taggart?" he asked.

"Yes, sir."

"You are in very serious trouble, young man."

I didn't need a judge to tell me that, especially in a case like this, where the cops went to so much trouble to set it up. They were out for blood. So I knew he was going to throw the book at me. I was hoping I wouldn't get sent up for more than twenty years. Twenty years? That would seem like forever. Why, I'd be an old man of almost forty when I got out—if I survived prison.

"Young man," the judge said, bringing me back to the present, "do you want help?"

I blinked. Why was the judge asking that kind of question? No, I didn't want help. I wanted out. But I knew there was no way I was going to get out of this one.

"Do you want help?" the judge repeated.

I turned to my legal aid and whispered, "What did he say?"

"He said, 'Do you want help?' I don't know what he's driving at, but don't stand there like a nut. Say yes."

I straightened up and answered, "Yes, sir."

Then I wondered why I let my legal aid talk me into that. Maybe the judge was trying to get people to volunteer for prison experiments, you know, where they reduce your sentence if you volunteer to be a medical guinea pig. I sure didn't want to do that. I'd heard of guys who were deformed from the experiments.

I thought I'd better qualify my statement, but while I was trying to frame the words, the judge said, "Mr. Taggart, there is somebody I want you to talk to. Then you'll be brought back to the court for sentencing."

I glanced at my legal aid. He shrugged.

A court officer took my arm and led me out of the courtroom, down the hall, and into a small room. "What's going on?" I asked.

"I don't know. I just heard that someone wanted to see you. I guess the judge knows what it's all about."

When I mentioned to him my fears about being a human guinea pig, he laughed. "Oh, no," he said, "nothing like that. That comes later—after you're in prison."

Relieved, I looked around. Any thoughts of escape were out of the question. The room had only one door—the one we came in. And the guard had told me he would be standing outside of it. The windows were barred—and we were five floors up. So what else could I do but sit and wait?

When the door opened, there stood another cop—a captain. I knew what he wanted. He was going to tell me that if I'd rat on Oscar and the rest of the guys, they'd reduce my sentence. Or maybe I'd have to go out on the streets with them and point out the junkies for them. No way was I going to cooperate!

"Can I talk with you a minute?" the cop asked.

Strange. Cops didn't usually ask. They told. Maybe he was trying to butter me up.

I turned toward the wall. "Listen, cop, you're not going to get me to rat on anybody. I mean, not one word."

He kind of laughed. "You have quite a temper, don't you?"

I wheeled around. "Listen, cop, I have my problems. I know that. I got busted. I know that. I'm going to get sent up the river. I know that. But there is absolutely no way that I'm going to go out on the street and do your police work. You got me, and that's all. As far as anybody else is concerned, that's your problem!"

I braced myself. I knew that any minute now I would feel his hand across my face. But, no! He just laughed again.

"Lefty, I know you know I'm a cop. But I want you to know I'm also something else."

Something else? Sure, he was a rat! A filthy, stinking rat! But I said, "Sure, sure. I suppose you're the mayor, too."

He laughed again. For a cop, he certainly had a sense of humor that most of them lacked.

"Besides being a policeman, I'm also a Christian," he said.

"A what?"

"A Christian. And as a Christian I am interested in helping young fellows and girls who are in trouble."

"Mister," I said, "you'll have to forgive me, but I'm just not following you. What's your game?"

"Lefty, let me level with you. My name is Captain Paul Delina, New York City Police Department. I am also treasurer of a fantastic organization called Teen Challenge. Years ago a minister named David Wilkerson started working among teenage gang members, then with drug addicts. His work came to be known as Teen Challenge. Well, I have been working with this organization from its very beginning. So besides my police work, I'm often able to help fellows like you."

That blew my mind. A cop trying to help the people he was arresting? I could never believe that.

"We have a nice home in Brooklyn where we help fellows," he continued. "After that, we send them to our farm out in Pennsylvania. Thousands of young people have been helped by our program. Today they are responsible, law-abiding, productive adults."

Teen Challenge? I'd heard of that somewhere.

"Officer, would you believe that a couple of weeks ago a reverend came up to me. Let's see, his name was Bennett, or something like that. He had something to do with a girls' home upstate."

"You must mean John Benton from the Walter Hoving Home in Garrison. Yes, that's a Teen Challenge home for girls."

"Well, he and this other guy named Victor Hernandez were on the street talking to us. Victor told me he graduated from Teen Challenge. He was really sold on that program."

"Yes, I've met Victor," the captain said. "He's a fantastic guy. He was really down in the gutter when he came to us, but he was completely changed by the power of Christ."

Changed by the power of Christ? What did that mean?

"There's someone else who wants to see you," the captain said.

He opened the door, and there stood my mother! She ran to me and threw her arms around me, hugging me tight. "Oh, Lefty! Lefty! It's so good to see you alive. Thank God you're alive!"

"Oh, Mom, of course I'm alive. But right now the future doesn't look too good for me."

She pushed back a little way. "Lefty, I've got news about your friend Oscar."

"Did they catch him?"

"Well, in a way; but he won't be going to prison."

"Hey, that's great! How did he beat the rap?"

"Lefty, he didn't. Oscar is dead."

"What?" I said in shock. "How? Where?"

"Lefty, it could have been you," she went on. "I guess the police cornered him in that apartment where the two of you lived. Oscar started shooting. The police tossed a smoke bomb in there. The next thing, his apartment was on fire. Oscar came running out with his clothes on fire and his gun blazing. They shot him."

I still couldn't believe it. Oscar had said they'd never take him alive. He must have gone back after our guns. And Mom was right. It was a good thing I hadn't been in the apartment, or now I would be dead, too.

"Now, Mrs. Taggart," Captain Delina said gently, "why don't you tell Lefty the good news?"

"I was coming to that," she said with a smile. "Lefty, while I was out looking for you after you ran out of our home, I really was discouraged. Nobody had seen you or knew where you were. I worried that you might be dead of an overdose in some burned-out tenement. Then I thought maybe you died in that fire in Oscar's apartment. I was just beside myself.

"Then one night as I was walking the streets, crying, this couple stopped and asked me what was the matter. When I told them, they said they were on their way to church and invited me to come along. I almost said no, but I figured that maybe it would get my mind off my problem for a while.

"The next thing I knew, we were sitting in a church. There was a lot of good singing and handclapping. I've never seen people so happy in all my life. But I was still thinking about you, Lefty."

"God's timing was just perfect," Captain Delina interrupted. "That evening we had a group from Teen Challenge in Brooklyn who gave their testimonies."

"Yes, and when those boys told what Jesus had done for them, I immediately thought of you, Lefty," Mom continued. "And I thought, *Wouldn't it be wonderful if my boy knew the joy these boys have?* Some of those fellows had been junkies, Lefty."

"But now they were free from dope because Jesus had changed their lives," Captain Delina said.

"Yes, and at the end of the service when the pastor asked for those who wanted to receive Jesus as their Saviour to come forward, I went up to the front, son," Mom said. "I gave my life to Jesus. And everything has been so different since then. I've been born again."

Mom did look different. She had a different smile—and a real sparkle to her eyes.

"Well, after the service, I saw this policeman"—she pointed to Captain Delina—"talking to those boys. So I went over and told him about you, Lefty—about how worried I was. And I asked him if I did find you, could I get you to their boys' program immediately."

"And I told her, she surely could," the captain said. "Then the next day I got a call from her and she was still worried about you. I told her to contact the courts—maybe you had been arrested. Well, that's how we found you. And that's why we're here today."

Well, it was nice of them to come. But at this point, what could they possibly do to help me?

"Lefty, the judge you have did me a big favor a few years

ago. A fellow named Sonny Arguizoni was handed over to me by that judge. Today Sonny is a minister out in California. He's got a big church, and with a bunch of other churches, has a tremendous farm for rehabilitation. He's one of the outstanding graduates of our Teen Challenge program. I believe God has given you this judge, because you and I are going out there and talk to him. And let's see what happens. Let's pray right now and commit this to the Lord."

The captain prayed. I don't really remember what he said. My mind was on one thing: freedom. I didn't care how I got out, I just wanted out. Anything would be better than Attica.

When Captain Delina said, "Amen," he signaled to the guard outside that we were ready to go back. We did, and about an hour later, the judge called me forward again.

"Lefty Taggart," he said, "I understand you have had a talk with Captain Delina and your mother. Do you think you would like to go into this Teen Challenge program?"

"Yes, sir!"

I wasn't about to say no to anything!

"Captain Delina, would you come and stand next to the prisoner, please?"

Almost immediately he was beside me, standing at attention.

"Captain Delina," the judge said, "I understand you specialize in helping difficult cases. I know that Sonny Arguizoni, whom you helped out a number of years ago, is now a minister in California and is doing very well."

"Yes, your honor," the captain said. "He and many others."

"So, Captain, I guess you've got another case on your hands," the judge said. "If you are willing, I will turn Lefty Taggart over to your custody. Will you take him?"

My heart was beating like crazy. A cop, responsible for me? How did he know—I might split just as soon as I got to the street. Why would he take a chance on me?

"Yes, your honor," Captain Delina said. "I'd be happy to take custody. I think Lefty is a fine young man with great possibilities."

The judge then turned his attention to me. "Lefty Taggart," he said, "you can thank your lucky stars for somebody like Captain Delina. He's most unusual. I hereby release you to his custody for one year. At the end of the year you are to report back to this court on your progress. That is all."

He slammed his gavel down and started shuffling some papers. I stood there, dumbfounded! And I noticed Captain Delina—he had tears in his eyes. Can you imagine that? A cop, crying!

Then out of the corner of my eye I caught a flurry of excitement as Mom and my little brother, Nicky, came running up. We all threw our arms around each other and hugged and cried and laughed. And I couldn't believe I was free!

I came to realize later that behind all this Someone was working in my behalf. I didn't recognize yet who He was. It was Jesus.

Nicky's face was wreathed in smiles. Had he gotten religion, too? It sure didn't take long to find out because he started right in on me: "Lefty, Jesus has wonderful plans for you. I know it!" I didn't realize what he was talking about, but I did come to know about those wonderful plans.

Outside the court building, I sucked in a deep breath of air. I can't describe how good it felt to be free—although I still didn't understand what freedom really was.

Next stop was Teen Challenge in Brooklyn. I guess Captain Delina had called ahead, because I had more fellows than I can remember slapping me on the back and telling me how glad they were to have me there. Then I met the dean of men, Randy Larson.

He explained the program to me. I'd spend three months in Brooklyn and then nine months on the farm in central Pennsylvania. And I'd have lots of Bible classes.

Just before I left Randy's office to be assigned a bed, he said, "Lefty, would you like to receive Jesus as your Saviour?"

What did I have to lose? If this Jesus had done something wonderful for Mom and Nicky, and He could do something for a crusty, old cop like Captain Delina, then maybe He could do something for a junkie like me. I didn't know all that it meant, but I said that yes, I would like to receive Jesus as my Saviour.

Randy then explained from the Bible what was involved. First, he said, I had to acknowledge that I was a sinner. That wasn't hard. Then I was to ask Jesus to forgive all my sins and by faith receive Him into my heart. He explained that that meant I really believed Jesus died for my sins and would come into my life when I asked Him to do it.

Then Randy led me in a short prayer which I repeated after Him. In it I admitted I was a sinner and I asked Jesus to forgive me. Then I told Him by faith I was going to receive Him into my heart.

Suddenly it happened! I felt so different—so clean, so new. And in that moment I knew—I mean, I actually knew—that Jesus forgave me. I had no doubt about it. I was born again.

I learned later that you're not supposed to go by feelings. When some people receive Christ, they don't feel anything. But I felt different immediately.

My dope habit? I'd gone through some pretty rough days

kicking cold turkey when I was in jail. But Jesus took all the desire for drugs away from me. I mean, it was an absolute miracle!

I spent three beautiful months at the center, and then they sent me out to the Teen Challenge farm. God continued to work in my heart, and I knew I was growing as a Christian. Through studying the Bible, I learned to take control of my life under the Lord's leadership. It was so beautiful.

Being at the farm was quite a change from the ghetto. Not only did I learn the Bible but we were also taught trade skills. You could study body shop, printing, mechanics, or farming. Because of that experience on my uncle's farm, I chose farming.

I had barn duty and learned how to connect the milking machines to the cows. They said I was one of their best farmers. Of course, I wasn't thrilled about cleaning out the barn. The smell reminded me of the ghetto!

Then the day came for me to graduate from Teen Challenge. Mom and Nicky, who had become members of the church where Mom first heard about Teen Challenge, came down for my graduation. I knew they were thrilled at the way I was growing as a Christian.

The next September I enrolled at Valley Forge Christian College in Phoenixville, Pennsylvania. God was calling me to be a preacher.

It must have been about the third day of classes, if I remember correctly. I was going down a hall between classes and for some reason turned my head. The next thing I knew I had bumped into this girl. My books and hers went everywhere.

I was so embarrassed. I mumbled an apology and stooped down, just when she did—our eyes met.

You're thinking it was love at first sight. Right? Wrong!

I looked straight into the eyes of Karen—Karen, the drug addict and prostitute from my old neighborhood!

"Karen, what on earth are you doing here?"

"Lefty Taggart! I was just about to ask you the same thing!"

"I went through Teen Challenge, and I've just come here to Bible school to study to be a minister."

That was all she could take. She threw her arms around me and cried. Then she said, "Lefty, I've been saved, too. I went through the program at the Walter Hoving Home— you know, the Teen Challenge girls' home. Now I'm studying here, too!"

Well, Karen and I met at the student union for coffee. We rejoiced together that God had been able to reach a couple of ghetto kids who had nothing to look forward to—humanly speaking.

I'm sure you can predict the end of the story. Four years later, Karen and I both graduated. And the next month after that we stood before a marriage altar and became husband and wife.

God has been so good to us. I pastor a church not far from Valley Forge Christian College. A number of the students attend there. Some, like us, are former addicts whom God has changed.

But what about you?

As you have read my story, you may also have been wondering about your own future. You may be like me, not really having any future to wonder about, grabbing what you can while you can. My future was probably to die in a shoot-out with the cops—as Oscar did. Oh, how close I came to it.

But God had something better for me. And He does for you, too. He didn't pick me out of the ghetto because I was someone special. He saved me and made me someone special. And Jesus wants to do that for you, too.

It can happen right now. Why don't you do what I did—what Randy Larson shared with me. First, just admit to God that you're a sinner. You know you are. Admit it to Him. Then confess your sins to Him. You don't have to name every one of them. Just tell Him you're sorry for all of them. Then receive Jesus as your Saviour by faith. It's simple. The Bible says: "If we confess our sins, he [God] is faithful and just to forgive us our sins, and to cleanse us from all unrighteousness" (1 John 1:9). Notice that if you do your part—confess your sins—He has promised to do His part and forgive them!

You can take my word for it. Jesus has a beautiful plan for your life, too. And today is the best day to begin it!

Some good things are happening at The Walter Hoving Home.

Dramatic and beautiful changes have been taking place in the lives of many girls since the Home began in 1967. Ninety-four percent of the graduates who have come with problems such as narcotic addiction, alcoholism and delinquency have found release and happiness in a new way of living—with Christ. The continued success of this work is made possible through contributions from individuals who are concerned about helping a girl gain freedom from enslaving habits. Will you join with us in this work by sending a check?

The Walter Hoving Home
Box 194
Garrison, New York 10524
(914) 424-3674

Your Gifts Are Tax Deductible

The Walter Hoving Home.